FLESH

WINNER OF THE

HEMINGWAY FIRST NOVEL AWARD

FLESH

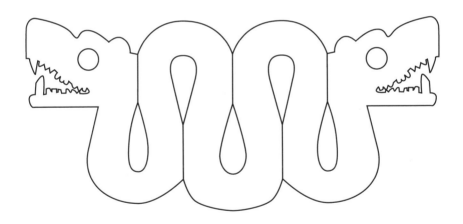

A NOVEL BY

RICK SKWIOT

Eaton Street Press, Inc.
P.O. Box 6006
Key West, Florida 33041-6006

FLESH

Copyright © 1998 by Rick Skwiot

All rights reserved. This book, or parts thereof, may not be
reproduced in any form without permission.

ISBN 1-884953-10-7

Library of Congress Catalog Card Number:
98-072443

Printed in the United States of America

Book Cover Design by Ellen Elfstrom-Perry
Cover Illustrations by Nancy del Aguila

To the memory of my father,

Edward Joseph Skwiot

Prologue

Nicholas Petrov stood with hands clasped behind him looking out from his glass bubble. That's how it seemed at times. Glass walls on two sides running floor to ceiling, no windows that would open, filtered air.

On the desk behind him glowing white words clung to a black screen and a telephone buzzed periodically. Twenty floors below, microscopic men scurried about and toy boats steamed down a gray river. A miniature freight train inched up a trestle to cross a bridge over the river, its black diesel smoke joining that of the boats and the chemical plants on the far bank. When the telephone fell silent a voice came from a speaker in the ceiling.

"Mr. Petrov, call the operator."

As the voice too quieted only a faint hum remained in the air, as though high voltage passed through the metal walls. No sounds from the ground came up through the glass.

"There you are, Nick."

He turned. A young woman in an efficient black dress stood in the doorway of his office.

"Why didn't you answer your page?"

He shook his head. "Didn't hear it."

She nodded toward the telephone and its dot of blinking white light. "It's your wife."

As he paced toward the phone the woman shook her head, pulled a half smile, and moved off down the hallway.

"Hello?"

"Nick. I've only got a minute. Don't forget we've theater tickets tonight."

"I thought that was Friday."

"Today is Friday."

When he made no audible response she said, "You're still thinking about him, aren't you?"

Phone in hand Nick turned back to gaze on the dismal scene outside the glass walls.

"What time?"

The river now shone silver-black and kept moving. Nick looked down at it through similar glass walls, those of his apartment. Reflected movement in the glass caused his eyes to focus there. He saw his wife sitting at the desk rolling cut leaf in a cigarette paper. She lit it, took a long pull, and held in the smoke. Nick refocused his eyes on the river and moved back into his own thoughts.

"Nicholas. . ."

He turned.

"You never did answer me."

When he wrinkled his brow and tilted his head slightly she added: "About beginning a family. It's time."

He studied her: thin, almost blonde, desirable. She didn't look near thirty though she was. Nick saw her glance at her watch, suck in one last stream of smoke, and carefully roll the ember from the half-burnt joint. She grabbed her purse.

"Half hour till curtain."

Nick wore the same gray flannel suit from the office. She wore black. The play was Strindberg, *The Father*. He watched the characters intently, allowing himself to be drawn into the drama of the stage household.

But then a line spoken by the wife to her officer husband made Nick turn to look at his wife sitting next to him. The woman in the play had planted a seed of doubt in her husband's mind as to whether he was the father of the child he had known for years. Nick studied his wife, not wondering whether he would be the true father of any child she might bear but, more broadly, whether he might trust her. Whether he might unreservedly entrust her with his child.

At that moment he noticed a thin, almost imperceptible line—just the slightest crease in her smooth, elegant face—running downward from the corner of her mouth. The precursor of an age line, he realized, unimportant in itself. But he also saw it as the beginning of a permanent, indelible sneer. An ever-present emblem of her distaste for life. A sneer at which Nick—and any child he might sire—would forever gaze. He turned back to the stage.

However, Nick now no longer saw there the captain and his wife but merely two actors plying their trade. The willful suspension of disbelief required to feel the emotion manufactured by the actors had been broken in him. And the line that ran downward from the corner of his wife's mouth seemed now to crisscross busily the glass bubble in which he lived.

One

The wind whistled up the rails toward the capital, chasing the Aztec Eagle over the black horizon. Sand, dust, bits of rock swirled around his legs, bit at his neck, and beat against the worn leather suitcase on the ground next to him. The breeze lifted the shirt from the sweat on his back—a remnant from the rancid air of the over-crowded train—and ripped a chill up his spine. But the chill was as much memory as anything: standing alone in the dark, knowing something was out there—if you could only see it. Maybe an enemy. A bad old memory. Nick left it.

He looked around. No light anywhere. No electric lamp, no moon, no nothing. Except for stars—the sky a deep blue velvet littered with iridescent lint.

But then along the horizon—merely a jagged black line where the stars stopped and total obscurity took over—he saw a white light sailing along. The headlight of a car or truck or. . .

"Damn." He spoke the word aloud.

Not a headlight, a satellite. Beaming America to savages. Or perhaps taking pictures. Nowhere to hide nowadays. He picked up his suitcase and chose a direction.

His shoes crunched over dry earth and wind rasped in his ear, but he could see little. However, soon a black shape began to grow in front of him, an area above the horizon without stars.

As he kept moving toward it the dark shape took form—the train station. No light there either.

He climbed creaking stairs to the platform and froze. Something there had moved. He called:

"Hay alguien allí?—Is anyone there?"

A light voice wafted back on the wind, "Sí, soy yo, soy yo. It is I."

Nick stepped toward the sound. Silhouetted against the starred sky he saw the profile of a girl. She sat alone on the deserted platform, books in her lap, legs dangling toward the tracks. The legs swung alternately back and forth: right, left, right, left, right, left. . .

"Were you on the train?"

He saw the silhouette nod.

"Where is the pueblo?" he asked.

"Not far—two kilometers."

He asked what she was doing sitting alone on the platform in the dark.

"Estoy esperando," she said. I am waiting. Or, I am hoping.

"Para qué?"

"Mi padre."

The girl patted the platform with her hand.

"Sit. My father will take you to town in his taxi."

Nick turned his suitcase on end, perched on it, and studied the girl, who sat with head tilted back slightly, watching the stars. None of his adult fear of menacing things in the dark. None of his history.

He asked, "Have you been on vacation?"

"No. I was staying with my aunt because my mother is ill. And you? Are you taking a vacation?"

He hesitated then said, "Sí."

The sound of a motor could be heard in the distance and soon two headlights came over a hill and lit the road running to the station.

The girl jumped up from the platform saying, "No one ever comes to Escondido for vacation."

As Nick approached the taxi he saw that the father was a dark, wiry Indian a good head shorter than he himself though perhaps his own age, maybe a few years younger. He took the suitcase from Nick without saying a word and opened the back door of the taxi.

They had driven in silence for a kilometer when the lights of the town appeared on the side of a hill. Nick asked, "Do you know a good hotel?"

He saw the driver's eyes flick up to him in the mirror then back to the road.

"Are you here for the antiquities?"

The little girl in the front seat turned around on her knees and stared at Nick. He looked at her and then to her father in the mirror.

"No, I know nothing of antiquities."

This time the gray eyes in the mirror rested on Nick for what seemed a long while before returning to the road.

Nick stood on the stone sidewalk looking the hotel up and down. A colonial structure perhaps three to four hundred years old and no doubt once an elegant home. But now dingy stucco flaked from the facade and paint peeled from its shutters. The sound of boisterous laughter came through a tall portal opening onto a dim courtyard.

"This is the best?"

The taxi driver handed him his bag.

"Es el único—It's the only one."

Nick paid the cabby and moved into the courtyard.

To his right he saw an ill-lit lobby of sorts: a four-foot-wide reception desk fashioned of stained plywood; a dusty wrought-iron chandelier fitted with cracked, flame-shaped bulbs; heavy wood-and-leather chairs. A threadbare Indian rug lay on the worn stone floor and a concrete stairway led, apparently, up to the rooms. The reception was unmanned.

To Nick's left on the far side of the courtyard three men sat at a low table that held Coca-Cola bottles, a liter of brandy, and glasses. Again the men broke into laughter while just beyond them a bored waiter leaned his elbows on a small, rectangular bar reminiscent of the reception desk. When he saw Nick, the waiter straightened. Then he moved quickly from behind the bar, crossed the courtyard, and slid behind the reception desk.

"Buenas noches."

He was a short, square-headed young man with shiny black hair flattened on his forehead. He looked up at Nick awaiting instructions.

"Una habitación, por favor. Your best room. With light. It must have good light."

The man nodded twice and lifted a key ring off a board behind him. He came around the reception desk.

"Número cinco. It has a terrace with much sun. Very pretty. . .Con permiso."

He grabbed Nick's suitcase and headed for the stairs. But as the short man put a foot on the first step a voice called from the courtyard, "Andrés!"

He stopped and turned. One of the three men at the table motioned to him.

"Perdón, señor."

Andrés set the bag down and recrossed the patio to the party of drinkers. He bent toward the heavy man seated in the center and listened nodding. When he returned to Nick he said, "Don Vicente invites you for a drink. I'll take your suitcase to your room."

Andrés lifted the bag once again and moved up the stairs without waiting for Nick to accept or decline the invitation. Nick paused then moved across the courtyard remembering that in Mexico one always had time for serendipitous invitations. Besides, after the hot train a beer was what he needed.

The three men rose, the heavyset one extending a hand.

"Welcome," he said in English. "I am Vicente Villas."

Nick took his hand. "Nicholas," he said and stopped there, staring at the man. A pleasant enough face—round, tanned, not unattractive. But half his mustache was missing: thick and black above the left side of his lip, clean shaven on the right.

The four men sat. The other two, younger and leaner than Vicente, were introduced as Luis and Miguel—but Nick had no idea which was which. Handsome young Mexicans with gold watches and neck chains, they said nothing, only nodding a greeting. It was Don Vicente who spoke.

"You are American, yes? The blond hair, the blue eyes. . .What would you like to drink? Brandy, tequila. . .?"

"A beer, I think. The train was hot."

Vicente motioned to the man on his right.

"Una cerveza para el hombre."

The young man got up and went behind the bar to fetch Nick's beer. When Vicente moved his hand to his lip and rubbed the bare skin there Nick realized he'd been staring again.

Vicente said, "I had forgotten. That witch Malena, she always escapes me. This time she takes my money, my watch, everything. And leaves me like this."

Nick poured the beer set in front of him and took a long drink from the glass. Vicente leaned across the low table to offer a cigarette. Nick started to reach for one reflexively, hesitated, then took it, and the fat

8

man lit it with a gold lighter. Then Vicente leaned back, lit his own, and stared off as though he heard voices. Finally he remembered the conversational thread.

"Ah. We were throwing dice at La Última Cena, in the back room. Malena cleans me out. I beg for one last throw. 'What will you bet?' she asks. 'You have nothing left.' I say, 'My mustache against your tarantula.'..."

When Nick frowned Don Vicente dropped his hand to his crotch to explain. "La tarantula es..."

"Pubic hair?"

Vicente nodded.

"But she says she cannot leave me with nothing, so she bets half her tarantula against half my mustache. But she never loses. Qué bruja!"

Luis and Miguel smiled at that. Qué bruja—what a witch.

Now Vicente smiled too. "And you, Nicholas. What brings you to Escondido?"

Nick shrugged. "I was traveling. I felt tired. The train stopped and I got off."

The smile vanished. "Then you know nothing of our artifacts?"

Nick shook his head.

"It is a special trade. Pre-Columbian figures. Permit me..."

Vicente produced a business card from his shirt pocket and passed it across. "Antigüedades de México," he said.

Nick studied the card then looked up. "I didn't know you could sell antiquities."

"Legally one cannot. At least not real antiquities. I deal only in reproductions—fakes. Some people might say forgeries. I have a fábrica outside town where we make all our artifacts. But we make no claims of authenticity. However, if some people chose to believe rumors that I also deal in protected artifacts and that what they purchase is the real item, that is their business.

"Many fine private collections and even some museums contain my pieces. If they are happy with Vicente's forgeries what difference does it make? Experts cannot tell my work from true antiquities without much scientific testing—and even that is unreliable. My statues and pottery use the same clay as the originals, are fashioned in the same traditional shapes, and are made by the same peoples. The only difference is that my Indians are not yet dead."

He laughed and Nick gave half a smile. Vicente continued:

"Besides, I am doing México a favor. If collectors are satisfied with my figures then the true antiquities can be preserved for the Mexican people."

Nick nodded. Real, fake; true, false. Such distinctions were always difficult, even more so in Mexico. He stood.

"Thank you for the drink."

The other three men stood as well.

"I've had a long day."

"Please come by my shop, Nicholas. It may be interesting to you."

"I'd like to learn more."

Nick again crossed the courtyard and climbed the stairs toward room number five, feeling the eyes of the three men on the back of his neck.

He flipped the light switch by the door. The room was narrow, clean, white. A high ceiling, a small desk, a semicircular brick fireplace in the corner.

His suitcase lay on the bed. He unlocked it and took out a book with a picture of an Olmec effigy on the cover, a book he had taken from his father's library. Nick placed the book on the crude wooden desk, turned on the reading lamp there, and leafed through the book until it fell open at the middle, where newspaper clippings had been folded inside. He riffled the clippings until he found the one he wanted and held it beneath the light.

The headline read, "Mexican's Art Is Legal, Lucrative." Printed below was a grainy but recognizable photograph of Vicente Villas with full mustache. Nick studied the photo and caption and reread the clipping, finding quotes from Vicente almost identical to his words in the bar. But that was all he could do now, just recover old ground. So he replaced the article in the book and turned off the desk lamp.

Next Nick undressed and, figuring he was too tired to read, turned off all the lights and slid beneath a gray Indian blanket covering the bed.

He lay in pitch blackness as, outside, church bells rang. He listened, eyes open. When the bells finally stopped, dogs began to howl. Strays—pariahs—perhaps, which were everywhere in Mexico. One had even crossed the runway when his plane landed. He waited in the dark, motionless, for the piercing cries to stop.

When after half an hour the howling had not abated he got up, switched on the desk lamp, and climbed back into bed— something he often did when death felt palpable around him and his inner self resisted sleep for fear of not waking. Now, in the glaring light, Nick was able to close his eyes and soon fell into a deep, dream-laced sleep.

■

He had not thought on it for years—if ever. But now the memory of it came in sharp detail, as though it had been only yesterday. . .The smell of damp earth in the air, the aroma of roots, dead leaves, and flowers. A man in a black frock coat rigid behind the polished wooden box, reading strange words from a black book, almost singing. His father stood above the box staring at it hard, like Superman when he wanted to use his X-ray vision. People had gathered round in black, silent, still, which frightened him, all the people he knew except for his mother who, he understood, lay sealed inside the wooden box. His father had told him that she was going away for good but also that she would always be with them. Nicholas, however, did not then see how that was possible.

He pulled his hand free from the grasp of the tall woman who held him and ran to his father, tripping over the canvas that covered the mound of dirt beside the hole in the ground. Nicholas righted himself, brushed soil from his palms, and moved to his father.

Once at his side he clutched his father's trouser leg, pressing himself against his father, looking up to him, waiting to be lifted in his arms. But Father made no move to him. It was as if he didn't even know he was there.

Then Nicholas felt hands on his shoulders and again smelled the flowers. The woman with the cold hands picked him up in her arms, touching her powdery face to his. As she carried him away Nicholas turned to look over his shoulder and saw the polished box being lowered into the earth. Then he felt a cold wetness on his cheek, tears from the powdery-faced woman, who placed her hand on the back of his head to turn it away from the grave.

But as they moved off together Nicholas craned to gaze over the woman's shoulder at the grave-side scene as if drawn to it, as though hopeful of understanding the meaning—if any—of death.

Two

Nick dreamed he was a monk lying on a pallet in a monastery cell as pealing church bells stirred him toward wakefulness.

He opened his eyes but the bells continued. Sunlight streamed through a circular opening high above his head in the thick wall. Covering him was a rough blanket, gray with a black design that looked like rows of dark wheat against twilight. A straight-backed chair sat in front of a rustic desk on which a book lay open, and Nick recalled the entire dream.

He had removed himself from the world—a monk whose lot was to sit at the crude desk copying over and over again the pages of an indecipherable manuscript. Nick closed his eyes to escape the vision but instead fell unconscious and returned fully to the dream. It was a colorless nightmare of isolation and endless toil over a codex whose meaning he would never know.

He threw back the shutters and froze as if he'd been slapped. Framed in the open window he saw a blue sky with cream-colored clouds over black mountains; a pastel pink steeple floated on a green sea of fir and avocado trees; magenta bougainvillea climbed the white wall to his terrace, where a window box cradled bright red geraniums. He pulled on his jeans and unbolted the door.

As he stepped out onto the terrace Andrés came up the stairs carrying a tray of coffee and sugared breads. The waiter set the tray on a cane table by a white string hammock and turned to share the view.

Nick gestured toward the steeple. "A beautiful church you have. Muy bella."

The Mexican put his hands on his hips. "Sí. The Church of the Inquisition. But now it is called the church of the soldiers."

"Christian soldiers?"

"Drug soldiers."

Nick turned his head toward Andrés, who continued:

"They stay in the old monastery when they're not out in the hills searching for the plantations, the factories, and the runners. When they catch someone. . ." Andrés lifted his chin toward the church's steeple. "… they bring him here."

"And then?"

Andrés shrugged blithely, as if he did not know and did not care. But then he shivered involuntarily and folded his arms over his chest to rub his shoulders as if suddenly chilled.

Nick moved beneath the hotel portal onto the stone sidewalk and gazed across the street to the zócalo, the town square ringed by neatly trimmed elms with white-painted trunks. In their shade motionless men sat on metal benches.

An old woman—face deeply lined, head wrapped in a soiled shawl—paused from her slow journey down the sidewalk and held out her palm to Nick. When he pressed a coin into it she asked God to bless him and moved off down the street on a whittled crutch. Nick strode off in the other direction.

He meandered over cave-like cobblestone streets contained by high Moorish walls painted every color. The town was small; he figured to find Vicente's shop sooner or later.

Compact, brown-skinned people stared as he passed. Seemingly Escondido lay far enough off the tourist routes that lanky blond Americans still seemed novelties.

The sun already hung high in the nearly cloudless sky and easily penetrated the thin mountain air. A light breeze brought aromas: the fragrance of flowers, the scent of cilantro, the stench of manure. As he turned down a narrow street the odor of rotting fruit engulfed him. Ahead he heard the braying of burros and the chatter of a crowd. At the next corner he saw the market.

Nick strolled among the stalls, ducking under canvases strung against the sun. He saw barrels of beans, black, brown, and white, and mounds of dried chiles, red, green, black. There were exotic fruits and nameless vegetables, plucked chickens with horrified eyes. Further on, colorful live birds squawked in bamboo cages—toucans and honey-creepers, parrots and macaws. At a stand where an Indian woman tended frying foods Nick bought a gordita filled with chorizo and cheese and ate as he walked.

At the far end of the market he stepped back into the sun reflecting warm off the colored windows of the church. His forehead damp, his mouth burning from the highly spiced sausage, he set off down the street in search of a beer.

At the next corner he spotted the faded blue half-doors of a cantina. Peering over the tops from bright sunlight, inside he saw a dark, cool bar. He pushed through the doors into the tavern, took a few steps, and abruptly stopped. An impulse to turn around and escape back out onto the hot street buzzed through him, but he saw it was too late. By the time his eyes had adjusted to the dim cantina light and he saw who was standing at the bar, he was already in. To leave now might mean problems later. So he smiled and nodded at the two men in the dark green uniforms and heavy black boots leaning against the bar staring at him and walked past them to the far end.

There he ordered a beer and kept his eyes trained on his own image in the mirror behind the bar. He had broken no law—but maybe that made no difference. He felt damn conspicuous and vulnerable. He sipped his beer and stared into the mirror.

Nick followed the reflection of the soldiers approaching. They stood behind him expressionless, still staring. The eyes of the fat one shone red and watery. The tall one's jaw moved laterally somewhat, as though grinding teeth. Nick managed to raise a smile and turned.

"Buenas tardes, señores. Much heat today. Perhaps you will permit me to buy you a beer."

The dark, stony faces broke into ingenuous grins.

"Muchas gracias, señor. Very kind."

Nick felt his shoulders drop in relief—just two bumpkins looking to cadge a drink. He signaled to the bartender for two more beers and shook hands with the soldiers. The fat one, Raúl, did the talking.

"To be a Mexican soldier is to starve," he said between sips of beer.

Jaime, who was nearly Nick's height but not nearly his weight, nodded. Raúl continued:

"We are paid fifty cents American per day, from which we must feed ourselves. There's a cook at the billet, but still. . ."

Nick shook his head. "It's not possible to live on that amount."

"Clearly," Raúl agreed. He leaned forward and breathed beer into Nick's face. "Perhaps you would like to buy some marijuana."

Nick took a sip of beer, noticing how plump Raúl had grown on fifty cents a day.

"No, gracias. I use no drugs. Only this." He held up his beer bottle.

"Yes, that is better for the health."

The three men clinked the three brown bottles together and drank to health. As Nick tipped his bottle back he noticed from the corner of his eye the fat one looking him up and down, sizing him up, as though he was someone Raúl wanted to fuck.

Nick turned to the bartender and called for one more round. That would be sufficient Pan-American courtesy, he figured, and kept smiling.

As he neared the zócalo Nick's eyes were drawn up to a sign hanging over the sidewalk: "Antigüedades de México."

The shop looked dark inside but he tried the door anyway without good result. He put his nose to the window, cupping his hands around his forehead to cut the glare. Inside, locked in glass display cases, he saw weathered statues, clay pots, and quartz effigies arranged in neat rows.

He leaned away and looked at his watch. Nearly two o'clock. Siesta. He would have to see Vicente later.

From a news vendor in the zócalo, Nick bought an *Excelsior* and read the headlines as he crossed the square. A corrupt official arrested, malnutrition on the rise, a smog crisis in the capital. It all seemed so familiar that he checked the date on the paper before folding it under his arm. Not what he needed to read himself into a peaceful nap. He spoke Spanish well enough, but reading it gave him a headache.

At the hotel Andrés handed him his key from behind the reception desk. Nick started to turn away then hesitated.

"Dígame. Tell me, Andrés. Do you know where I can buy books or magazines in English?"

18

Andrés stroked his chin and shook his head.

"Or perhaps borrow them?"

After a beat Andrés' eyes widened and he thrust a finger into the air.

"Come. Follow me."

Nick tailed the short man across the courtyard to the bar, behind which Andrés squatted and began rummaging through stacks of old newspapers.

"What are you looking for?"

"For what you wish, señor, books in English. Some were left behind by the dead gringo."

Nick's eyes tightened. "A dead gringo?"

"Sí. A man with silver hair."

"How did he die?"

Andrés stood, clutching a stack of four books. He blew dust from around the sides, wiped the top book with his shirt sleeve, and shrugged.

"One day yes, one day no."

Andrés dropped the books heavily on the bar and Nick started, feeling a cold hand pass across the back of his neck. Dying alone in some backwater Mexican town. . .

He studied the spines of the books. Walt Whitman, *Myths and Symbols of Pre-Columbian Mexico*, Turgenev's *Fathers and Sons*, a Bible.

Nick picked up the Bible, opened the cover, and inside read the name written there in a careful and elegant hand:

Alexander Joseph Petrov.

He set the book aside, conscious that his fingers trembled.

He then laid open the mythology book on the bar top, where he could steady his hands, as Andrés silently watched. Noticing that the corner of a page had been folded in, Nick turned there, to a translation of an Aztec hymn underscored lightly in pencil.

> *Be ye happy under the flower bush, many-colored like*
> *the quetzal bird.*
> *Listen to the quechol bird singing to the gods.*
> *Listen to its flute by the river in the house of reeds.*
> *Would that my flowers might never die.*
>> *Our flesh is as flowers;*
>> *flowers in the flower land.*

He closed the book and thanked Andrés.

Nick crossed the courtyard to the stairs with the books under his arm, making a silent vow not to be buried in Mexico like his father.

■

The childhood incident returned to him now with a new poignancy and power. . .Church bells in the distance, the noise of traffic on the street, the call of a newspaper vendor: "Excelsior!" Young Nicholas sat straight up in bed rubbing his eyes with the backs of his hands then squinting against morning sunlight. Looking about the room he remembered now where he had been brought. Dark, heavy furniture; red drapes over an open window; an unmade bed beside his; light coming through the bathroom door. In an ashtray on the night stand a matchbook read, "Hotel Géneve, México, D.F." He called toward the bathroom:

"Father. . .Father!"

When he heard no response, he padded barefoot in striped flannel pajamas from the bed to the bath but found it unoccupied. Nicholas ran to the hotel room door and used both hands to pull it open.

Empty hallways ran left, right, and straight ahead. Again he called for his father and again no answer came.

Nicholas moved off in search of him, following the hallway to his right, which turned and met yet another hall. That led to another, which intersected one more still. There he stopped, looked about him, and moved to retrace his steps. He ran back down the hall. But when he got to where he thought his room was, there was no door. Biting his lip he turned and called:

"Father! Where are you?"

Silence answered his plea. Again he set out, running through the maze of halls with dark doors, all shut tight, struggling to fight back tears forming in the corners of his eyes, fearing that now his father had also abandoned him.

Tears blinding him, he sped through the hallways turning corner after corner calling for his father. Finally Nicholas ran headlong into a woman carrying an armload of towels, the starch of her white apron coarse against his cheek. He looked up to her brown face as she held him at arm's length, looming over him like a dark, menacing bird, her shadow falling across his face. Her lips began to move.

"Qué haces niño? Donde vas tan rapidamente?"

Nicholas, his bottom lip quivering, understood nothing, could say nothing in reply. Without a word he pulled away from the woman, turned, and bolted, racing through the labyrinth, fearing he had lost his father forever.

Three

Nick lay suspended in the white cord hammock strung on the terrace, swinging slowly, eyes fixed on an orange sun falling behind black mountains. The clouds now sat pink and pleated on a cobalt sky; a sliver of moon rested perfectly in a seam. White egrets glided from the sky to settle in for the night atop tall firs beyond the church. A scent of jasmine hung in the still air.

The unreal colors, the thin air, and the movement of the hammock combined to heighten in Nick a feeling of detachment—but a feeling wrought by more than just physical sensation. As he swung his feet to the cool, tiled terrace, the motion stopped. Too much thinking. That, too, made him dreamy and inert. He promised himself more discipline in the future.

He padded inside, slipped his feet into dusty sneakers, and pulled on a khaki jacket. Locking the door behind him as he left, he moved down the stairs and laid the key on the reception desk.

Nick crossed the zócalo hardly noticing the few people scattered there and wandered aimlessly through darkening streets, concentrating on the cobblestones, trying not to twist his bad ankle. Saturday night and the town seemed emptied. Few windows were opened onto the streets, doors shut tight. Behind the walls were people and light, he assumed, but in the streets only he and the darkness.

As he walked on he heard a low growl ahead and looked up. Then from the shadows a gray pariah leaped, snapping and snarling. Nick jumped back, jerking his hands up to prevent them from being bitten. A filthy, piebald animal, it barked, showed yellow teeth, and again moved toward him.

Nick backed against a wall searching for something with which to ward off the dog. He bent to pick up a stone and as he did the animal suddenly turned and slunk away into the dark. Nick stood, still clutching the stone. Somewhere the stray had been taught a lesson.

He let the stone fall to the ground and strode on alone. But the town seemed dead, the streets like catacombs, so he wound back to the zócalo, where he knew there would be at least some life.

At the square he strolled hands in pockets counterclockwise under the elms alive with the "kik-kik-kik" of great-tailed grackles. Now young men had gathered on the benches, eyeing groups of teenage girls circling the zócalo hand-in-hand.

However, Nick noticed all this only peripherally, for his eyes stayed largely on the ground in front of him. He had promised himself not to think too much on things but saw he wasn't doing a good job of it. Then a voice made him look up.

"Señor. . .Señor."

At the sitio in front of him the driver who had brought him from the station leaned against his green and white cab. The door of the taxi stood open with the radio playing softly, the sad sound of an accordion floating out to Nick. The cabby frowned.

"Estás bien, señor?"

Nick nodded. "I'm okay."

"Yet something worries you."

"Nothing I can change."

"Sí, I know how it can be. At times a man feels things running around inside and doesn't know what to do about them. I have found only one way to calm them."

"What's that?"

"You truly want to know?"

Nick nodded. "De veras. Tell me."

"I will show you. Ven."

Nick wedged himself into the front seat of the cab and the driver started the engine.

"They call me Francisco."

The two men shook hands.

"Nicholas."

They stopped at a confectionery to buy beer. Once beyond the city limits Francisco killed the radio. They cruised sipping in silence, windows rolled down, balmy night air blowing in their faces. The smell of the night and the taste of the beer, the speed, the sudden feeling of freedom, made Nick feel a twinge for something lost.

They sailed along the bumpy highway, Francisco pointing out a farm where one could buy good pulque, then mountain tops shaped liked a woman, and the road to the rancho where his brother bred horses.

"His ranch is rustic," said Francisco, "but the countryside is very beautiful. Whenever you wish, Martín will lend you a horse. If one does not know the campo one does not know México."

A few kilometers out of town Francisco veered off the highway. After another kilometer down a dusty path he stopped the taxi. Through the windshield Nick saw a series of low mounds, level on top.

"Toltec pyramids," Francisco said, "covered by time. Come."

Nick followed him to the far side of the largest mound. With his cowboy boot Francisco kicked away a dry shrub at its base, behind which Nick saw a dark opening. Francisco took a cigarette lighter from his pocket, flicked it on, and ducked into the darkness. Nick, feeling a sudden chill at the prospect of entering the tomb, hesitated. But he had no acceptable choice but to follow.

Inside was a low room that seemingly was indeed some sort of ancient crypt—but whether a Toltec pyramid or not Nick had no idea. Whatever might have once been sealed inside had long since been looted. Francisco raised his lighter toward the wall.

"And here are the ancient paintings." But as the wall became illuminated the taxista muttered, "Ay, cabrón!"

The crude paintings of animals, men, and sacred symbols that had existed intact for a thousand years had been spray-painted over with the name of a Mexican pop singer. Nick took in a long breath and felt his stomach rise at the sacrilege. It settled back down and he leaned closer to examine the partially obliterated glyphs.

"Look, Francisco. The serpent," Nick said. "An earth symbol."

"And here. . .here is Miquitzli," he added, pointing to the representation of a skull. "The deity of death."

Francisco studied the wall then looked to Nick. "You know much about my fathers. Where did you learn?"

Nick was studying the outline of a jaguar. "From my father."

Nick looked around the crypt as he stood hunched, his head touching the ceiling. He sucked his teeth.

"It's all gone—the vessels, the jewelry, the dead."

Francisco nodded. "Robbers. Many years ago it is said. Now at times a farmer will turn over a pot or a statue with his plow. But that's all that is left."

Nick moved back outside through the low opening, Francisco behind him. They climbed to the top of the mound, where Francisco opened two beer bottles and handed one to Nick, who stood with head back, staring into the heavens. Francisco crouched at his side.

The only sound was the wind. Nick saw no light except that of the moon and stars. Standing atop the pyramid he was surrounded by them, feeling enveloped and at the same time overwhelmed by the vastness. The universe was too big to fathom; he—and his worries—small.

"Tienes razón, Francisco. You are right. This stops that thing running around inside my chest."

After another silent minute Nick heard a noise and looked down. Francisco was hissing softly and staring at something in the distance.

"What is it?"

"Pinches satélites!"

Nick followed Francisco's gaze to the horizon, where a white light sailed along through the stars—a recent and dubious addition to the heavens. Nick silently agreed: fucking satellites.

Francisco said, "Tell me, Nicholas. Your father, how does he come to know so much?"

"He lived with discipline."

"And you have done the same?"

"Not so much."

The cab driver watched Nick gaze off into the distance as though again searching for the satellite.

"He is dead now?"

"Now he is dead."

Francisco offered Nick a cigarette from a pack in his shirt pocket and again struck the lighter.

"It is both bad and good when a man's father dies."

Nick looked at the Indian. Francisco went on:

"A father's death means something more than whatever a man feels for his father. As long as he lives, you cannot die. You are safe. But once he goes there is nothing between you and that." He gestured toward the dark emptiness of the sky with his beer bottle. "Then you see there is much to be done and only so much time. That is the good part."

Nick sucked at his beer. That was the feeling he had all right. But it did not yet feel good to him.

The townsfolk had once again abandoned the zócalo by the time Francisco dropped Nick there.

"Hasta el lunes."

"Bueno. Until Monday, Francisco."

The cabby drove off and Nick stood alone in the peaceful square.

A few campesinas, perhaps come to town for the market, slept with their children under the portales surrounding the square. The grackles had quieted. The church bell rang ten and fell silent. Nick strolled across the zócalo in no hurry to go upstairs to his dark and quiet room.

He stopped on the sidewalk in front of the hotel, cocked his head, and stood perfectly still. A faint sound of music came to him on the night air. He turned and stepped into the street and now could hear it better. Not a radio nor a record player—too vibrant for that. Soft, piquant sounds. He moved off down the street following the music.

Mindful of missteps and pariahs Nick covered two dark blocks, which increased the volume of the music, but then made a turn that diminished the sound, so retraced his steps and tried again.

Soon he turned a corner where the music became much clearer. At the same time he saw a shaft of yellow light cutting in two the street ahead of him. He now got a better take on the music, which seemed more Brazilian or Cuban than Mexican. He moved toward the light.

It came through an open doorway beneath a sign that read "La Última Cena"—The Last Supper or, perhaps, The Superior Dinner—and bore a lacquered reproduction of Leonardo's painting of Christ dining with his disciples. Nick stood in the doorway and gazed inside.

Down three steps lay a cellar lit by tall candles on long wooden tables where people clustered on narrow benches, drinking, eating, talking. In the corner on a low platform a band of young musicians banged out the Latin music: flute, African drums, Spanish guitars, an old double bass. In front of the band couples jammed a small dance floor and moved to the music. Nick tried to catch the lyrics shouted out by the band over the talk and laughter but as best he could tell they sang that Jesus Christ was in fact Peruvian.

On the far side of the room near the dance floor he spied a bar with young men three deep in front of it. Nick moved down the steps and headed there.

The smooth rhythm of the music made his walk feel weighty and awkward. He also felt a hundred eyes on him, and so moved as quickly as he could across the room, turning sideways to slide between tables.

At the bar he found a gap where he could lean in and call to the bartender for a beer. Then Nick turned, put his back against the bar, and looked around him. Everyone had stopped staring and gone back to their drinks—that is, everyone except for two men at the end of the bar, Don Vicente's men Luis and Miguel. Nick nodded. They may have nodded back but he wasn't sure. He looked past them to the dancers.

Partners faced each other without touching, hands held near the chest. They stepped lightly and smoothly back and forth, moving en masse to the music as seeming pieces of a whole.

But then at the center of the body of dancers he saw a woman moving alone—not out of synch with the music but seemingly moving to a deeper, more complex rhythm. She wore a sleeveless red dress that fit tight around her hips. "Serpentine" was the word that came to Nick's mind. Straight black hair, light bronze skin, stoic demeanor.

A descendant of both Conquistador and Indio, a lovely reminder of the true nature of the Conquest. She glanced up to Nick with a look of surprise.

Perhaps she had felt him staring. And he loomed half a head above the other men at the bar, who now turned to see what had distracted her, glimpsed Nick, and turned back to the woman. She seemed to sense them watching and recomposed her other, harder face. Then she came forward, pushing through the dancers. The men at the bar parted. She moved between them, coming straight for Nick.

Her scent arrived first, musky perfume and perspiration, earthy and good smelling to him. The red dress clinging to her damp body appeared to be all she was wearing, that and sandals, and she seemed near naked to Nick. As her hollowed hips moved to the music, her breasts pressing softly against the dress, she reached out a hand toward him.

The music filled his head and pulsed in his chest. His eyes drank in the fetching woman in front of him whose hand beckoned, but still he could not move. He hesitated, feeling an awkwardness in his inner-most being and a sudden, unaccountable fear, as if she beckoned him toward something dark and unknown.

Then he felt a hand in the middle of his back pushing him forward (the hand of God, she would later claim). He grasped her hand and let himself be pulled onto the dance floor.

There Nick became part of the undulating mass as best he could while his eyes measured the young woman in front of him. Her body seemed youthful and firm. But the damp dress sliding over it produced a sensation of great fluidity, which made him think that her flesh might be malleable in his hands. Her black hair fell without curl to her shoulders and was cut straight across a high forehead. The cheekbones he saw were Indian, as were the lips; the nose straight and

Spanish. The eyes, large and Moorish, remained fixed on Nick's face. He saw her lips move.

"Me recuerdas. . ." she began, but then stopped mid-sentence.

He leaned forward. "I remind you of whom?"

She shook her head and closed her eyes as if driving the thought from her mind. Then she opened them and looked him up and down.

"The way you move pleases me."

He said over the banging of drums, "No, it is you who move beautifully and pleasingly. Besides, I never before danced like this."

"No importa lo que ha pasado antes. Ahora empieza."

What passed before is not important. Now it begins, Nick translated to himself, but felt he was missing an idiom that held deeper meaning.

Then she danced close to him, leaning forward as if about to elaborate. He inhaled again the warm fragrance of her and felt her hot breath on his cheek, but she said no more. Nick stared into nearly black irises then dropped his gaze to the pinched waist and the long hips still moving to the music. She so preoccupied him that this time he did not feel the eyes of Don Vicente's men on the back of his neck.

He bent to light a candle on a three-legged stool that served as his night stand, turned, and saw her standing rigid by the foot of the bed, arms held at her sides.

Nick moved to her and let his fingertips graze her bare arms. She shivered, closed her eyes, and bent back her head to receive a kiss. He brushed her lips with his, laid his hands on her hips, and gathered the dress up to her waist. She raised her arms above her head and he lifted the dress over them, keeping his eyes on her body.

He had been wrong about her being naked beneath the red dress. She wore a thin black bikini and, from a leather thong around her neck, a jade amulet hung between round breasts. The nipples were dark and drawn and firm to his touch as he pressed them softly with his palms.

Nick pulled off his tee shirt and saw that she was lifting the thong from her neck. She stood on tiptoe and reached up to place it over his head.

"I give you Kukulcan," she said, "the snake that can fly and leave its earthly existence."

Now, for not the first time since he left, he thought of his wife. There had been no other woman since they married and now this one was going to be the first. Whatever that meant he pushed out of his head along with any thoughts of her. He wanted nothing thoughtful nor abstract nor meaningful now. Mere earthly existence was sufficient.

He pulled her easily onto the bed where she lay motionless on her back staring at him. He slid the dark bikini down over her hips, down her thighs, over her ankles. He pulled off his trousers and knelt beside her.

Though her skin had seemed light in contrast to those around her in the dim tavern, he now saw that she was much darker than he. Her flat bronze stomach moved in and out with deep breaths. Nick looked up and saw her eyes searching his face—almost as if she was afraid.

He kissed her breasts and her stomach and traced his fingers up between her thighs to the triangle of black hair. She parted her legs and he moved on top of her.

He put his hand behind her knee and lifted it. Then he parted the wet labia with his fingertips and moved his hips forward.

The eyes that had been fixed on him suddenly closed and she

clenched her teeth. When he felt the pressure against him, Nick stopped and leaned back. She opened her eyes.

As he knelt beside her staring she tried to pull him forward. But he resisted.

"You are a virgin."

"It is not important."

"I believe it is. It is for your husband."

"We have come together now for a reason."

He moved his head slightly from side to side.

"There is no reason for nothing."

She squeezed his hand. "Then come."

"I can promise nothing."

"Come."

She lifted the other knee as well, laid an arm across his back, and with the other hand grabbed him and pulled him inside, raising her hips to meet his and giving a muffled cry as he broke into her.

Now Nick moved slowly in rhythm with the woman in his arms, the jade Kukulcan dangling from his neck between her dark breasts. Outside he heard the bell from the Church of the Inquisition begin to chime the hour, and the pariahs began to howl. Then Nick heard his own voice breathing her name as though an incantation: "Malena... Malena... Malena."

■

An unfettered sun beat down on him as in the distance creamy white clouds blew across the horizon from the Pacific. Nick stood atop the ruin in his baseball cap looking down into the valley of Oaxaca, pretending that he was a Zapotec king leading his warriors in one last, futile stand against the advancing Mixtec conquerors, fighting unto death to protect the holy city of Monte Albán.

"Nicholas! Nicholas!"

At the base of the temple steps where he made his valiant defense, his father stood gesturing for Nick to join him. Nick descended grasping his golden machete, slaying Mixtecs on the way down.

"What do you make of this, Son? Notice."

With the stem of his pipe his father indicated the outlines of stylized human figures carved into the stones ringing the temple—nudes, with limbs askew and bodies misshapen.

"They all look like cripples."

His father nodded. "Very good. They do appear to be disfigured. Why do you suppose the Zapotecs adorned their religious sites with such deformed human representations?"

Nick thought. He remembered the pyramids at Teotihuacan with their carved serpents. And the statues of jaguars at the museum in Mexico City. Animals that the Indians worshipped. That must be it.

"Because they're gods?"

His father pursed his lips. "Perhaps. Perhaps they do represent Zapotec deities. But that's unusual, isn't it? Normally gods embody strength, vigor, human perfection. Why would the Zapotecs worship deformity?"

That one was tougher and made Nick think harder. But thinking was difficult on such a day, with the high sky and brilliant sun, with ancient ruins all around and the checkerboard of lush fields in the valley below. It was easier to think at home in the winter when everything was gray, when you couldn't go outside and there was nothing to do. But he knew that if he gave a good answer his father would leave him alone for a while. So he thought as hard as he could about gods. It was then he remembered something Father Bob had said in religion class, about man being made in God's image. Nick felt confident he'd hit on the answer.

"Because the Zapotecs were deformed."

His father smiled and laid a hand on his son's shoulder. "Maybe. Maybe. At least perhaps the priestly class. That would make sense."

When his father lifted his hand, Nick was off.

He ran down the ball court—where, his father had explained, the Zapotecs played a game not unlike soccer—and kicked a goal with an invisible ball. From there he moved to the far side of the largest temple, which abutted the shrub-covered slopes surrounding Monte Albán. As he was about to scale the side of the temple to lead another defense of the holy city he heard a hissing in the foliage behind him.

As Nick turned, a small, dark man wearing a white straw hat and carrying a cloth bag on his shoulder emerged from the underbrush with hand extended.

"Se vende una antigüedad verdadera. Lo mismo como ellos en el museo."

In his palm he held a stone figure of a bow-legged deity with feathered headdress. A true ancient artifact, Nick had understood, just like those in the Museum of Oaxaca, where his father had taken him that morning. The man held the figure out to him, urging him to take it. Nick did, turning it in his hands. It sure looked like the ones in the museum.

"Where did you find it?" Nick asked.

In the field behind his house, the man answered, where he was digging a well. He went on:

"Por favor, Señor. I wish I did not have to sell it. I wish I could give it to the museum. But I must buy milk for my children. I do not want much money, only enough to feed my family today."

Nick looked from the figure in his hand to the wiry man in front of him, no taller than Nick himself. He tried to imagine the children who had no milk and in his mind's eye saw ragged, barefooted urchins in front of a makeshift hovel, just like those he had seen outside Mexico City. Nick bit his bottom lip.

"I don't have much money."

The man looked disappointed, his shoulders suddenly drooping.

"How much?"

Nick handed back the figure and dug into the pocket of his blue jeans. Finally he fished out three pieces of crumpled currency and held them out to the man.

Looking into Nick's palm the dark man seemed, if possible, even more despondent. "Is that all?"

"Sí. I'm sorry."

The man took a deep breath and shrugged as though in resignation.

"Pues, está bien," he said lifting the money from Nick's hand and replacing it with the stone figurine. When Nick looked up from the bowlegged deity the man had already retreated back into the brush.

Nick found his father still squatting before the carvings of the deformed people on the temple exterior and ran up to him with his find.

"Look, Dad!"

His father rose and took the figure from him, turning it in his hand.

"Where did you get this?"

"From a man who found it digging a well."

"Of course."

"It's a real antiquity!"

"Hardly," his father said, handing it back to Nicholas and returning his attention to the temple carvings.

Nick felt his heart sink. It had to be real. The poor man had told him so.

"How do you know? You don't know everything."

His father turned his gaze on his son.

"I know disrespect when I hear it."

Nick swallowed hard and studied the figure in his hands, trying to hold back his tears, knowing he was too old now to cry when reprimanded. "I'm sorry."

"Very well. Now I will tell you how I know. How much did you pay for it?"

Nick shrugged. "That money you gave me this morning."

"Twelve pesos. A dollar and a half. Nothing valuable comes cheaply, Nicholas. Remember that."

"Yes, sir," Nick answered.

And his father again turned away to resume his study of the deformed deities.

Four

As the wind rattled the shutters above the desk Nick looked up from the Turgenev lying open beneath the desk lamp. The logs in the fireplace cast an orange glow on the white walls and thickened the air with the aroma of mesquite. He picked up a glass of brandy from the desk, sniffed it, and sipped. How good it was to have his brandy, his fire, his book, and his solitude.

He had slept past noon despite the bells ringing Sunday Masses and when he awoke Malena was gone. Andrés then brought from the kitchen eggs with jalapeños, which Nick ate in the sun on the terrace. Dark clouds came late in the afternoon along with a wind that seemed to carry the first feel of autumn.

Nick set down the brandy and returned to the Turgenev. But soon something he read—a conversation between Arcadii and his father, Nicholai—made him put it aside and reach for the book with the Olmec effigy on the cover. He opened it, took from it a letter typed on embossed stationery, and read it once again, flipping it over to scan the attached documents. Nick made a mental note of the signatures there, those of Chief of Police Rafael Hernandez on the death certificate and, on the autopsy report, Dr. E. E. Sanchez.

As the fire popped, a knock came at the door. Nick replaced the letter and the documents in the book, closed the book inside his suitcase, and went to the door.

"Quién?" he called through it.

The wind again shook the shutters and swished through the trees and somewhere nearby a cat cried, but there was no answer.

He cracked open the door and a shaft of orange light from the fire fell on a dark, hooded figure who moved toward him. Nick took a quick step back then saw Malena's eyes beneath a black shawl and breathed out. He let her pass, closing the door behind her.

She wore a long-sleeved black dress and her coffee-brown eyes seemed almost as dark. Standing close, she stared up at him and something in her look made the back of his neck tingle. She touched her hand to his.

"Ven. Come with me."

He frowned. "Has something happened?"

She stared at him. "Sí. . .No. There are things we must know."

He put his hand to her cheek. "Relax by the fire, Malena. Have a drink."

She shook her head. "Don't worry, Nicholas, but please come." She squeezed his hand as if to reassure him.

Nick looked at the fine fire he had going, then grabbed his jacket and threw back the remainder of his brandy.

At the bottom of the stone stairway he heard conversation and glanced across the courtyard. Don Vicente waved. He sat at the low table with a white-haired couple: a woman with hair cropped short, a man with a trimmed white beard. On the floor next to the man sat a travel bag. Nick waved back and, as he and Malena crossed to the reception, recognized the hissing sound of English coming from the trio.

Nick hooked his key on the board behind the reception desk and said to Malena, "You know Don Vicente, sí?"

"Más o menos."

The wind gusted across the deserted zócalo, bending the elms. Malena took Nick's arm and held herself close as she led him across the square. He felt her shaking, as if spooked by something.

They moved through the dark streets without speaking and soon were walking down a long hill away from the town center. They crossed a bridge over a foul-smelling creek and picked their way over a dirt road past shacks of stone, bamboo, and brick. The wind whipped dust into their faces and blew thick, low clouds across the sky. Nick turned his head sharply to the right at the howl of a nearby dog, feeling Malena's fingernails dig into his wrist.

"We are not far," she whispered.

They turned up a path worn through scrub and weed that soon gave out in a grove of trees, beneath which sat a crude stone house. Nick saw flickering yellow light behind a cloth hanging over a doorway and, as they approached, noticed a smoky, herbal smell that reminded him of Oaxaca, where his father had taken him as a boy, and the huts where Mixtecs sold mescal.

Malena called through the covered doorway.

"Itzél. . .Itzél."

The trees stirred noisily. A deep, female voice came through the curtain.

"Pasa, Maria Elena."

As Nick stooped and followed Malena through the curtain he saw immediately why they had come. Dark fabrics draped the walls. Candles had been positioned throughout the room in front of painted images and figurines, the icons surrounded by flowers and dried stalks to create small altars. But these were not Christian altars; the paintings and carvings depicted strange beasts, feathered men, and corn. At a small, round table covered by a purple cloth sat a wrinkled yet handsome woman. She wore a dark silk shawl on her shoulders. Wavy black hair streaked with gray tumbled onto the shawl. Her eyes were still and deep and her smile peaceful—or insane. Nick knew that she, too, was a witch and that they had come to see the future.

The old woman stared at Nick as he and Malena sat on either side of her. When he stared back unblinkingly she turned to Malena. Itzél laid weathered hands on the table palms up, Malena grasped them, and the old witch's lips began to move as though mouthing an oft-repeated prayer. Finally, closing her eyes, she began to speak aloud.

"You will live with fierceness, Malena. I see much heat, much light in your life. The fire that has been without air will now breathe. But know that the straw that burns bright burns quickly."

The old woman opened her eyes. "Now, daughter, is there a question, something special you wish to know?"

Malena gazed at the old witch, nodding. "Sí. Tell me of my heart—will it be granted its desires?"

Itzél closed her eyes once more, still clasping Malena's hands. Nick could hear the heavy breath of the old woman, who began slowly to nod.

"Yes, Malena. All that your heart wishes will be yours—for a time."

Malena smiled, swinging her eyes to Nick, who did not feel so confident in the old woman's prophecy. When he looked back to Itzél she was holding out her hands toward him. Staring into the deep, lunatic eyes of the old witch, he hesitated. But then he reached across the table and placed his hands in the soothsayer's. After all, it was just mumbo jumbo, without validity. So he might as well humor Malena, knowing no harm could come from it.

The hands of Itzél felt warm and dry and her gray-brown eyes seemed to penetrate him. Nick sensed something sexual pass between the old witch and him. No doubt she'd once been a beautiful woman.

Again her eyes closed, again the mumbled prayer as the candlelight cut hard shadows into her face. Soon her shoulder seemed to twitch and a frown came to her brow.

"Your hands. . .They have known death. . ."

He thought of the autopsy report and death certificate he'd just handled, and he thought of the war. Her clairvoyance seemed vague. But then the lines in her forehead deepened.

". . .and they will again—soon."

He saw Malena look at him. Nick licked his lips and tried to swallow but found that his throat was too dry. After a moment the witch continued:

"The one you left is forever in the past. Take care not to live there but to begin again."

That would be Regan. But most men have a past and usually there's a woman haunting it. However, the word "forever" summoned to him again the old woman's death prophecy—which he again pushed aside. Hell, it was all just superstition. Still, he didn't like that part.

She opened her eyes. "Now, señor, what more? Is there a question about the future—or about what has passed?"

Nick looked from the witch to Malena pursing his lips. She nodded to encourage him.

"Anything," the witch said. "Something that bothers you, something you do not understand, or. . ."

Then it occurred to him. He turned back to the witch and spat it out without thinking.

"Sí. The old gringo they buried here last month. Tell me how he died."

The witch's eyes narrowed as Malena's opened wide, and she gazed at Nick with lips parted, as though seeing him now for the first time.

She asked him about it as they walked back up the hill.

"Who was he? Did you know him?"

Nick answered without looking at her, "Andrés gave me books the gringo left behind. I was curious."

He left it at that though he could still feel her looking at him. But he kept his eyes straight ahead as they walked and said no more and soon she looked away.

The band at La Última Cena had not yet started to play but the men at the bar were already shoulder to shoulder. Nick called to the bartender over their heads for two brandies. The wind, the witch, and her chill words made Nick want something warming. Your hands will soon again know death. Ha. Of course there was nothing to it. But still he felt cold inside.

A young man standing in front of Nick and wearing a checked shirt and high-crowned straw hat turned. He looked from Nick to Malena and back again then stepped aside and gestured toward the bar.

"Por favor, señor. Pásale."

"Gracias."

As Nick moved to the rail for the drinks, he saw that the man who made room for him was drinking dark beer so he bought him one.

"Muy amable—very kind," the stranger said when Nick handed him the bottle and he resumed his place at the bar. The three of them raised their drinks.

"Salúd!"

He was a thin, sun-darkened man of perhaps twenty-five who, Nick saw, wore sharp-toed boots and narrow jeans.

"Do you work on a ranch?"

The young man nodded. "A grand ranch in the other valley. By horse, two hours from Escondido."

"Hard work?"

The cowboy offered cigarettes to Malena and Nick from a pack of Faros on the bar. Malena shook her head but Nick accepted a thin, oval cigarette, held it to the proffered match, and inhaled smooth, strong smoke.

The cowboy said, "We work from dawn as long as there is light and on Sundays we come to town."

When the band began to play, Malena tugged at Nick's arm. They set their drinks on the bar next to the cowboy and moved to the dance floor.

Nick watched Malena move easily and elegantly to the samba-like music, deciding she looked best in black. The sexy red dress she'd first worn had also flattered her slender figure and dark visage, but he preferred now the feeling of severity the black gave her, making her seem more serious, less approachable, and thus more valuable. Though he wasn't sure he'd feel the same if he hadn't already slept with her.

He studied Malena, imagining the movement of her flesh beneath the black dress, but also noticed the cowboy. As soon as the music had started, the vaquero went to a table where three young women drank cubalibres and took the prettiest to the dance floor. The sun came up early Monday morning.

As the samba ended, Malena led Nick back to the bar while the cowboy stayed on the dance floor. She sipped at her brandy, eyeing Nick, her gaze making him uncomfortable.

"What are you thinking?" he asked.

She hesitated then said, "You are not a man who has come to rest, nor to hide. You are like a hawk, searching."

Not a hawk, he thought, a vulture come for human carrion. But then his eyes were drawn toward the street, where Vicente's two men were entering through the open doorway and strutting down the three steps into the tavern. They came to the bar where the cowboy had stood, pushed his beer and cigarettes aside, and lifted their chins solemnly at Nick. He nodded and turned back to Malena.

"Don't worry, Malena. If I am searching, it is not for another woman."

"No, but when you find what you want you will leave."

As the band finished the song and began another the young man from the rancho returned, leaning around Luis and Miguel, searching for his beer. One was pointing a finger at the other's chest and speaking in rapid whispers. The cowboy coughed.

"Con permiso, señores."

They ignored him, as though he did not exist.

"Permítame," he tried again. "If it is possible for one to move aside…"

The one being lectured to—Luis, perhaps—turned to the cowboy. "What do you want, shit shoveler?"

From behind, Nick could see the cowboy's ears redden and his body tense. But his voice remained calm.

"Excuse me for bothering you, lords, but that is my beer on the bar."

They handed it to him.

"And those are my cigarettes."

Those they passed across.

"And one other thing."

He waited until both turned and glowered at him and he had their full attention.

"That is my place at the bar where you two sons of whores are standing."

Nick took a few steps back and pulled Malena with him.

The one on the left moved first, swinging out with the glass in his hand and landing it behind the cowboy's ear. As the cowboy lunged for his attacker's throat, the band stopped playing and the room filled with shouting and the sound of breaking glass. Soon Luis and Miguel had the cowboy on the floor, kicking at him, and he wrapped his arms around his head. The other men at the bar jumped in, carefully pulling the two off the fallen vaquero. They made calming gestures with their hands and spoke to Luis and Miguel as one might to fractious stallions.

A crowd encircled the cowboy on the floor. Soon the flash of a red light made Nick turn toward the street. Through the doorway he saw a paunchy man in a beige uniform pry himself from the passenger seat of a small police car and move down the steps into the tavern as though entering his favorite bordello. He sauntered across the room smiling at the women, patting the younger girls on the shoulder, shaking hands all around. His driver followed at a distance, carrying a long nightstick. The officer approached the bar tugging on the belt of his holstered revolver and shaking his head.

"Jóvenes, jóvenes. . ." He turned to the band and raised a hand into the air. "Música!"

As the band began again to play, he moved close to Luis and Miguel and began to converse with them, scratching the back of his head. But with the music Nick could not hear what was being said.

Meanwhile the cowboy had picked himself off the floor and tried to reshape the crown of his hat as blood trickled from his ear. The officer at the bar turned and motioned to the cop with the nightstick, who walked up to the cowboy, clamped handcuffs on his wrists, and led him toward the door. Don Vicente's men turned back to the bar to order fresh drinks and the officer with the revolver walked past Nick, waving good-bye to all.

Nick looked to Malena. "Qué pasa?"

Malena shrugged. "The police have made an arrest; the fight is finished."

"But they arrested the wrong man."

Malena wagged a finger at him. "No, they arrested the Indian. Such is life."

Nick shook his head. They all looked Indian to him.

"Does the chief of police know how his men operate?" he asked.

Malena motioned with her head toward the well-fed officer retreating up the steps. "That is the chief, Rafael Hernandez."

Nick walked Malena to the door of her casita where he told her he was tired and kissed her goodnight. He'd had enough for one night—too much. He wound his way back to the hotel with his collar turned up against the wind, watching for stray dogs and thinking of omens, prophecy, and sudden violence.

The hotel lobby was empty except for the night porter, who handed him key number five. Once upstairs Nick bolted the door of his room behind him. He undressed, took the Turgenev from the desk, and climbed into the bed that still held her scent.

He had read only a few lines when his eyes began to close. He fell lightly into a dream of gaudy flowers falling from the sky like brightly colored parachutes—yellow, blue, red, green. Atop a red silk parachute Malena floated down. Then a door slammed, Nick started, and the Turgenev slid from his chest to the bed beside him.

Words—English—began floating to him, seemingly from the shower. He heard a man's voice, then a woman's.

"Don't you think. . .?"

"Yes, yes. Excellent. Mayan, most definitely. Of course he had to claim it was fake, but. . ."

Nick remembered the two white-haired gringos talking with Vicente in the bar and smiled. Real, fake; truth, illusion. He closed his eyes and went back to watching the exotic flowers fall.

■

Nick came from his bedroom and moved down the hall past the kitchen and dining room to the living room, where his father sat in an over-stuffed chair, legs extended, head back, a book lying open on his chest. In the air hung the scratchy voice of a woman, a voice familiar to him for his father had played the record a hundred times. Wagner, Nick knew, but which opera he did not know and did not care.

He stood between his father and the black and white television waiting for the aria to end. When the hi-fi fell momentarily silent except for the rumble of the needle in the groove, Nick said, "Dad. . .Can I watch now?"

His father opened his eyes, lifting his left eyebrow, to study his son. The orchestra resumed its play.

"You've finished your homework?"

Nick nodded.

"What did you do?"

"A report on European history."

Nick stood fidgeting.

"May I ask on which aspect of European history?"

"The Battle of Britain."

"Let's see it, Nicholas."

"But 'Combat's' starting."

Now his father raised both eyebrows at his unruly son and Nick checked himself. No arguing, no whining, no petulance—or risk a dark, bottomless wrath whose mere threat chilled him. Expressionless, without further utterance, Nick turned toward his bedroom to retrieve the report.

It lay on his desk beneath his pen, under the green glass lamp shade, and he quickly sat to proofread it one last time. "Parliment"—that didn't look right. He corrected its spelling against the encyclopedia lying open on the desk. Nick added a comma between two independent clauses and concocted a transition to begin the concluding paragraph.

His father had turned off the hi-fi and sat at the dining room table with reading glasses on his nose. He took the paper from his son and read nodding silently, raising an occasional eyebrow, asking once for the pen to correct a pronoun problem Nick had missed.

Nick held his tongue, anxiously yet surreptitiously peering at the clock on the kitchen wall, awaiting his father's pronouncement on the paper. Finally it came.

"As I've said before, Nicholas, you write well. But you need to dig deeper into your subject. You're only skimming here, just reporting facts without any analysis, without any explication of their significance."

Nick felt his heart sink and stole another glance at the clock in the adjoining room.

"But I bet I'll get an A."

His father took the reading glasses from his nose and grasped his son's hand in his own.

"I'm sure you would. But we have to grade ourselves as well. Are you doing your best? Are you gaining understanding? Are you finding yourself in your subject?"

When Nick shrugged his father explained.

"What I mean is this, Nicholas: To discover the truth you must dig. That is what I do, both literally and figuratively: I dig. Into the earth, into the past, into myself.

"There's a Mayan legend of the man-god who journeys to the underworld in search of his father's bones. Once he has found them he returns to the world of light, armed now with the wisdom of the past and the knowledge of himself and

his forebears." He released his son's hand and pressed his forefinger into the boy's chest. "You too must dig in this rich soil to find the treasure buried there."

Nick nodded, not daring to risk another look at the clock, knowing that at this point, once the old man got going on digging up old bones and dead Indians, it was hopeless.

Five

The clouds had disappeared during the night and the morning air was calm. Nick had draped his shirt over the back of a sling chair on the terrace and sat taking the sun.

The Turgenev lay in his lap but face down. Nick was enjoying the slow, unforced waking, letting the sun do it. He thought of days upon days of buzzing alarm clocks and nicked upper lips—a daily blood sacrifice of which the Aztecs might have approved.

The sound of a door opening and being squeezed shut made him open his eyes. The man with the white beard and the travel bag—now slung over his shoulder—had emerged from a neighboring room patting the pockets of his bush jacket. Satisfied, he turned to cross the terrace and finally noticed Nick.

"Ah, good morning!" Then he looked over his shoulder at the door he had just closed and moved away from it. He continued, lowering his voice.

"You're the other gringo in town, I understand. Vicente pointed you out as you passed last night."

The man spoke an archaic-sounding American Nick could not place. He looked like he came from another century as well: neat beard, lively eyes, eccentric movements.

At the sound of footsteps on the stairs both men turned to watch in silence. Andrés' head appeared.

"Buenos dias, señores. Quisieran café?"

Nick turned to the other American. "Will you have coffee with me? Good. . .Sí, Andrés. Dos cafés y pan dulce."

When Nick turned back, the man was staring at him as though mesmerized. Nick nodded toward the hammock.

"Have a seat."

The words seemed to break the spell. The man unslung the shoulder bag and lowered himself gingerly into the center of the white net hammock.

"Excuse me for staring but I was admiring your amulet."

Nick looked down to his bare chest and the jade hanging there. "A gift from a Mexican friend."

The man again stared and put the fingers of his right hand to his lips.

"Do you mind if I. . .?"

Nick lifted the leather thong over his head and handed it across. The man took reading glasses from his coat pocket and placed them on his nose. He held the amulet up to the sun, turning it back and forth.

"Kukulcan. . .Do you know him?. . .The Mayan representation of Quetzalcoatl, the plumed serpent, the sun god. A blond god, some say. Probably a real man, an ancient king. The great civilizer.

"But the symbolism is what's interesting. Quetzal, the rare green bird; co, or snake; and atl, water. Sky, animal, and earth. A ladder to the gods, from the underworld to the heavens. . .This is a very nice piece."

Andrés returned with the sweet rolls and a pot of coffee and set the tray on the low cane table between them.

"Y nada para la señora?"

The man shook his head. "Ya está durmiendo," he said with the same American accent, gesturing to show that she still slept, as if mistrustful of his Spanish.

Andrés nodded and disappeared down the stairs. Nick poured the coffee and handed the man a cup. He in turn passed the amulet back to Nick and folded the reading glasses away in his coat.

"You see that sort of dualism throughout the mythology here. A snake that can fly, matter that can metamorphose into spirit. . ."

He took a sip of coffee and went on:

"That's what makes these people so damn difficult to understand. They won't hold still. Everyone's elusive, everything's something else eventually—intangible yet permanent. No, the plumed serpent is no abstract god nor accidental myth. It is Mexico.

"For example, the flowers on Kukulcan's headdress," he said nodding toward the amulet, once again strung around Nick's neck. "Living matter carved into dead, inert jade. A seeming contradiction. But a reminder. Life is ephemeral, all life must perish. Only death is permanent."

A deep buzzing sound made both men turn. An iridescent green hummingbird hovered at the purplish bougainvillea climbing the wall behind them then darted away.

Nick sipped his coffee. Then: "Are you a friend of Don Vicente?"

The white-haired man pursed his lips and shook his head. "No, no. Only a customer. We bought a few pieces at his shop yesterday."

"Antiquities?"

The man smiled and again shook his head—but faster this time Nick thought.

"He sells only fakes. Recreations. Vicente has a factory outside town where he manufactures the figures. But they're good fakes and they've even fooled some museum people.

"His business is entirely legal if not entirely ethical. He knows his forgeries may be passed off later as the real thing. Since now there's no legal trade in antiquities coming out of Mexico, often they go first to France or Switzerland then are sold to American buyers as coming from old European collections. All very sophisticated and very fraudulent. But Vicente himself is within the law."

The man stood. So did Nick, and as they shook hands the man's eyes fell once again to the amulet on Nick's chest.

"Where did you say the jade came from?"

"From a friend. I don't know where she bought it."

"Well, if she did buy it she did so illegally—and probably paid dearly for it. That's the real thing you have around your neck."

Nick finished his breakfast and looked at his watch. He dressed hurriedly, trotted down the stairs, and crossed the zócalo. As he did, a car with posters of tigers and big-breasted women in leotards taped to its doors circled the zócalo. Loudspeakers on its roof announced, "The Magic Circus is coming to Escondido!"

On the far side of the square Nick found Francisco leaning against his taxi chewing on a toothpick. They shook hands and climbed into the cab. Francisco headed the taxi back out past the edge of town to the highway that had carried them to the pyramids.

Francisco drove in silence, Nick watching him chew nervously on the toothpick.

"Como estás?"

"So-so." Francisco looked out the side window then turned back and flipped the sun visor down in front of him. "My wife Barbarita still is not well."

"Has she seen the doctor?"

The taxi driver nodded. "Yesterday."

"What does he say?"

"He says she will be better in a few days."

"Is there anything more to be done now?"

Francisco shook his head.

"Then don't worry. The doctor is taking care of her."

Martín's ranch was as Francisco had characterized it: rustic. A small mud-brick house painted white, an old stone stable, chickens strutting among a dozen horses in a makeshift corral. But it sat near the mouth of a ravine where a clear creek emptied into a blue lake surrounded by pale green willows.

As they closed the doors of the cab Martín looked up from underneath the hood of a battered white pickup. He reached through the open window of the truck to turn off the engine then embraced his brother.

"Pancho, Pancho."

After he shook Nick's hand Francisco told him why they had come.

"Bueno." Martín wiped his hands on an oily rag. "I'd rather be with my horses than work on this damn machine."

They followed him to the stable, where Martín saddled three horses and shot questions at Nick.

"Do you know Los Angeles?"

"Do you have a swimming pool?"

"Is it true all gringas are whores?"

When the horses were saddled the three men headed them up the ravine.

Soon hundred-foot-high cliffs leaned over them on either side. Along the creek where the horses walked, grew leafy shrubs, flowering cactus, and Mexican cypress. In the high sky Nick saw silhouettes but could not tell whether they were hawks or vultures.

"When it rains," said Martín, "and all the water from the mesa comes running through this arroyo, it is like Genesis."

Martín was older, taller, and broader than his brother, as well as more talkative. Nick figured that came with living alone in the countryside.

The horses followed the creek for half a kilometer to a waterfall at the head of the ravine. White water poured from the high rocks and fell through rainbows with a steady roar.

Martín urged his palomino up a steep, rocky trail cut into the side of the ravine, Nick and Francisco following. At the top they came to a vast, treeless mesa. The brothers kicked their horses and off they went.

The two Indians stretched low along their horses' necks, racing across the flat land and disappearing down a hidden gully. Nick followed, letting his chestnut mare lope easily across the mesa.

When he came to the gully the horizon dropped and Nick pulled on the reins. In the distance a crucifix floated above a coffee-colored ridge. Then he realized what it was: the cross atop the spire of the Church of the Inquisition. They had been riding south and were only a few kilometers from town.

When Nick caught up with the brothers they were resting their horses in the shade of a spiny mesquite tree and looking out over an adjoining ranch marked by a high hurricane fence with rolls of barbed wire laced on top. Well beyond the fence sat a red-roofed hacienda.

Nick also dismounted. Martín took binoculars from a leather bag tied alongside his machete on his saddle horn and handed them to Nick, who focused the glasses on the hacienda.

"What is it?"

Martín answered, "The ranch of Vicente Villas. You know of him? Look to the left of the casa and behind it. That's the fábrica where they make the artifacts. On the other side is a stable."

Nick swung the glasses to the right. He saw a blue truck and beyond it another building.

"Vicente breeds horses as well?" he asked, lowering the binoculars.

Martín scratched his chest between the buttons of his blue shirt.

"I've never seen a horse on that side of the fence. It is a rancho without horses."

"What do you see on that side?"

Martín shook his head.

"I do not look because I do not wish to know."

The three men mounted and turned the horses around.

"Come," said Martín. "I'll show you places with no fences. Then, at comida, you can tell me the truth about life in the United States."

Nick smiled from the side of his mouth.

"I will do that, hombre, but you will not believe me."

■

Nick felt nearly nauseated by the stale air of the apartment, and a surge of anger grew within him. He laid his book face-down on the desk and tiptoed to his bedroom door. Cracking it open he gazed to the dining room where, beneath a hovering cloud of blue smoke, his father and Dr. Kaminski leaned over the chessboard, each clutching a long-stemmed briar pipe. When Kaminski reached up and moved his bishop across the grid, Nicholas's father leaned back lifting his eyebrows and muttering an oath in Polish.

Sundays were the worst. Mass with the émigrés, dinner at the cafeteria where his father would grill him about his lessons, then this—afternoon study hall—because his grades were never what everyone thought they should be. "Does not make good use of time," his report card always read. He thought he might someday have it inscribed on his tombstone, Nick once told his disapproving father, and got the back of a thick hand clapped sharp on his ear for his cynical witticism. The thought of the incident made Nick feel even more angry—and rebellious.

He eased the bedroom door open, sidled through it, and crept across the dim hallway to the kitchen. There he inched open the door to the fire escape and slipped outside. As he did, the damp January cold hit his face like a slap and slid under his sweater like an icy hand. Nick's coat hung unreachable on a hook by the front door, but he should have thought to take a jacket from his closet. Too late now he told himself, racing down the metal stairs two at a time.

Hands in pockets Nick crossed the backyard patch of brown grass and pushed through the wire gate into the blood brick alley starred with bits of broken glass. There he broke into a loping run. He turned left at the end of the block, moving up the street toward the school yard.

The sky—flat, steely, low—pressed him toward the earth; a chill, wet, stinging wind swept in from the west. As he neared the school he spotted a cluster of boys on the lone field pushing against one another then falling to earth.

"Hey, there's Nick! Even sides!"

Someone threw him the football and he passed it back expertly. But Nick preferred defense, where he could run full speed at an opponent and drill him to earth, where he could be aggressive and solitary, without the confines of a planned play. In the school yard he particularly enjoyed knocking down Golden Boy, as they called the tall, arrogant WASP who always had to play quarterback, to whom all the other guys in the neighborhood deferred, and whom all the girls loved. Nick managed to get a good shot in on him during the first series.

Soon Nick's team had the ball and it came to him in the right flat on a short pass. He tucked it under his outside arm and raced down the sidelines, using his left forearm and fist to ward off tacklers. Nick cut back across the grain of the pursuit until downed in the middle of the field, falling hard to the frozen earth beneath a pile of players. Someone ripped the ball from his arms and kicked weakly at his head. Nick jumped up, fists clenched at his sides.

Golden Boy loomed above him saying, "You can't do that. You can't punch people."

"The fuck I can't," said Nick, moving to stand chest-to-chest with Golden Boy but knowing it was folly to fight him, who had two years' growth on Nick.

Golden Boy sneered, "What do you know, you stupid Polack?"

Nick tore into him, clawing at his face, trying to rip it apart. He kicked at his shins and tried to knee his groin in hopes of sterilizing the bastard. A hot rage burned in him, and like a cornered animal Nick flailed viciously.

But after its initial surge his undisciplined ferocity weakened against superior strength. Sharp punches fell to his eyes and jaw and he felt himself going down, on the edge of consciousness.

His ill-conceived aggression finished, Nick lay on the cold earth trying to regain his equilibrium and pull himself up, feeling isolated and dejected, though not because of the fight. There he had stood his ground and taken his beating. But he knew that when he finally managed to limp home, his wrathful father would be waiting, sitting in harsh judgment, seething with disapproval of his wild, undisciplined, and star-crossed son.

Six

The sun beat down on Nick's neck and dirt caked to his lips where they met. He moved in a cloud of dust with Malena, who clutched a brown paper package to her chest, and other pilgrims. He had asked about the package earlier that morning, when she first came up to the terrace and found him in the hammock drinking coffee.

"Tortillas and chiles for our lunch," she had answered. "Today is the Day of the Dead and we are to dine with my father at his grave."

Along the road to the panteón, vendors hawked fruits, candies, and small sugar replicas of human skulls with names hand-printed across the foreheads. Nick searched without success for someone selling beer. The dust and the sun made him thirsty. But he also felt shaky, like he needed a drink to steady his nerves. He had purposefully stayed away. And now, unexpectedly, he was going with Malena.

The wide band of mestizos and Indios stretched out in front and behind as if marching off to work the fields. Nick tried to imagine what it had been like for them before the revolution—tried to imagine himself among slaves being herded to the Yucatan to harvest hemp— but could not summon up any credible facsimile emotion. Nor could he imagine the lives of the thin campesinos and underclass townsfolk he marched with now.

A bottleneck at the cemetery gates slowed the pilgrims but soon Nick and Malena shuffled through into the graveyard. Just inside the walls, in the shade of tall poplars, he saw austere women in pressed black dresses and polished black shoes tending to white marble crypts. The women decorated the crypts, which sat in cool, green grass, with food, flowers, and photographs of the dead.

Malena located her father's grave nearby. As she knelt beside it and folded her hands Nick moved off down the hill.

Near the center of the graveyard he passed a priest celebrating Mass, laying the body of Christ on outstretched tongues—which made Nick think again of cold beer. He continued on further down the hill.

Soon he found himself among plain concrete crypts standing four high in the sun, the names and dates of the dead printed seemingly with fingertips in the once-wet mortar sealing the crypts. Here, too, families crowded around their dead to share with them a meal.

At the back wall of the cemetery Nick saw children playing on a mound of broken, mud-caked coffins—some made of thin sheet metal, some of wood. Nearby he noticed a grizzled old gravedigger who had just begun a new grave.

"Buenos dias."

"Buenos dias, señor."

"Tell me," said Nick, indicating the deteriorating caskets piled against the wall. "Why are those no longer in the ground?"

"Porque no pagan la renta."

Nick nodded. Behind in the rent; evicted.

"And the bones? What happens to those?"

The old man made a quick gesture, an upward movement of his hand over his shoulder. Out with the other garbage, he seemed to say. Nick had no more questions.

"Gracias."

As he moved away he felt a crunching beneath the soles of his shoes and looked down to a pile of bones that had pushed up through the earth. He recognized a tibia and wondered how deep the old man buried them.

Surrounding him Nick now saw dusty, unkempt graves baking in the unbuffered sun, some without markers, some with simple wooden crosses. One seemed still fairly fresh—the ground had not yet subsided nor been beaten smooth by hard rain. As he stepped closer he saw the word "Petrov" lettered clumsily in black paint on a raw pine cross.

Nick looked up and about him, turning away, hands in pockets. He heard the voice of the priest—bits of barely audible and incomprehensible Spanish—fading in and out on the breeze. His eyes again fell on the disinterred coffins stacked at the back of the cemetery.

He had known he was here but sensed it wouldn't be good and so had stayed away. But now. . .Nick fell to his knees beside the grave, plucked a bottle cap out of the dirt there, and tossed it aside. Hands resting on his thighs he took in and let out a deep breath. Then he stood and walked away, stopped and came back. Again he knelt, grabbing handfuls of dirt. He sat motionless, staring at the grave for long minutes, seeing his father in his den, at the dinner table, at a dig in his straw hat, and, finally, as he last saw him, standing on the stoop of his flat, waving his last goodbye to his ungrateful only child.

Nick looked again to the wooden cross. Petrov. The name had always seemed to suit his father better than him, seemed so Old World. His father had clung to the European values of *his* father—the ideals, the discipline, the old-fashioned morals—and Nick had done whatever he could to distance himself from that. He had rebelled against his father's authority, discarded discipline, and eventually eschewed books for business—one hundred percent Americano. Against his father's wishes he went to war and married a professed Protestant whose American ancestors owned slaves while his people were still vassals. Nick remembered how, when he was fourteen and about to begin high school in another part of the city, he had enrolled as Nick Peters. When the priest telephoned about the discrepancy, his father said he would pay the tuition only of Nicholas Petrov. Nick now crossed himself, stood, and brushed pale dust from the knees of his jeans.

When he rejoined Malena at the top of the hill he saw that she had spread a white tablecloth atop her father's low crypt and arranged their meal on it. Nick looked at the headstone:

Emiliano Escorza Ruiz

21 Mayo 1928 a 18 Enero 1989

An old man to have such a young daughter.

Malena sat on the shaded grave, hands folded in her lap. As he sat next to her she handed him a tortilla wrapped around a chile.

"My father was a simple man," she said. "He liked campesino food."

Nick looked down the hill feeling a sudden desire to have a beer with his father, to sit by his grave and talk. Likewise, all around him families had gathered at the graves of their dead. He recalled what the bearded gringo had said the previous morning about life being ephemeral and death permanent. Eventually, they would all be reunited—in body if not in spirit.

"Nicholas. . .Nicholas."

Malena sat staring at him with eyebrows knitted together.

"I'm sorry," he said shaking his head as if to dispel his thoughts. He dwelt on death while Malena—so very much alive—sat before him. She had worn the black dress again. He gazed at her tan legs disappearing into it and thought of her thighs. "Lo siento. It is finished. I'm with you now."

"Bueno," she said smiling, but then lowered her eyes and asked, "Who is there, in the grave in the sun?"

So she had been watching. He studied her. No, he didn't know her,

64

didn't know how much to tell her. You hope to be able to trust the woman you sleep with—but then he thought of his wife.

Finally he said, "This is only for us, between you and me—like other intimate things about which we do not talk to others."

"Of course."

Nick's gaze moved off down the hill. "It is the grave of my father."

She stared at Nick, eyes moving slightly from side to side as though trying to understand but not succeeding. At last she spoke:

"Then our fathers are together for eternity, as we shall be."

Nick looked at her not knowing how to respond to her prophecy— if that's what it was, or, more likely, just wishful thinking. He decided to avoid it altogether.

"Enough talk of death. We are alive and honor our fathers best by living fully and with intensity," Nick said, realizing these were words his father might have spoken.

She smiled and nodded and looked so beautiful and happy that he decided not to tell her he had no intention of leaving his father's body in a Mexican grave, to be thrown out with the trash.

Outside the cemetery she wrapped her arm through his as they moved among the makeshift stalls of the vendors who sold intricate sugar sculptures of human skeletons marrying, drinking tequila, and riding skeleton burros.

"This is the true Mexican art," Nick heard someone say in English and looked up to see the white-bearded American and his wife making a purchase at the next stall. Nick exchanged greetings with them and moved on with Malena, fingering the amulet beneath his shirt.

"Malena, tell me. The Kukulcan you gave me, where did you get it?"

She turned away from him as they walked and said, "I don't remember. Perhaps from a friend."

When she refused to look at him he said, "I answered your question about the grave in the sun with honesty. I wish the same."

Malena stopped at a booth and pretended to admire a sugar skull with black-painted teeth. Turning it in her hand she casually said, "I won the Kukulcan playing dice, from Don Vicente."

Nick took the skull from her and handed it across to the vendor.

"This one please. With the name 'Malena'."

She unlocked the door of her casita and carried the skull with her name printed across the forehead to the mantel above the fireplace as Nick closed the door behind him.

It felt cool within the heavy bricks of the small house. He saw a wooden table with two chairs, straw mats and cushions spread about the floor in front of the fireplace, and Indian weavings decorating peach-colored walls.

He crossed the room and stood behind her at the mantel. Malena cradled the skull in her palms and gazed smiling into its eye sockets. It was difficult to imagine Malena as a skeleton. No smooth brown skin, no muscular legs, no dark, liquid eyes—just brittle bones like sugar paste.

She placed the skull on the mantel between a ceramic statue of the Madonna and a gold-framed photo. Taking the photograph in her hand she pointed to a girl on a pony next to an army officer on his horse.

"This is me, and this is my father. Es muy guapo, sí?"

"Yes, very handsome," Nick agreed, but the snapshot showed only a man with a sombrero pulled down over his eyes.

"And your mother, is she alive?"

"Sí."

She said the word quickly and, he thought, coldly.

"Where is she?"

"De Efe."

D.F. El Distrito Federal—Mexico City. But that answer too was clipped, so he asked no more questions.

As he put his arms around her from behind, she folded her hands over his. After a moment she unfastened the top two buttons of her dress and placed his hand inside.

He pressed her breast with one hand and moved the other down the front of her dress and between her legs. When he stroked her up and down there and put his lips on her neck, she leaned her head on his shoulder and let out a soft moan. But when he looked up, he saw that her eyes were still fixed on the picture of the man on horseback.

The sun was setting behind dark clouds that approached on the horizon as he slipped out the door from Malena's casita. Nick wound his way toward the zócalo with the fragrance of her still on his hands and his lips. He also carried with him the remnants of sleep, of the deep siesta they had fallen into together after sex.

The sky turned brilliant red as he walked, the scent of a jasmine bush wafted to him on a light breeze, and he had the sensation of sleepwalking, as though he strolled through a dream. But not exactly. Though it did not seem quite real—lacking the drab familiarity he had long associated with consciousness—neither did it feel totally surreal. But, rather, super-real, vibrantly real, like a memory of childhood. The vivid life he now lived in Mexico made everything that had passed before seem like a monochromatic trance from which only now was he awakening.

As he turned a corner he saw a lighted window beneath the sign "Antigüedades de México." He moved to it and looked inside. A teen-age girl behind the counter polished what seemed to be a piece of jade. When Nick stepped through the open doorway she looked up.

"Buenas tardes, señor."

"Buenas tardes. I am looking for Señor Villas."

She locked the jade inside one of the glass display cases.

"Momentito."

The girl disappeared through a doorway covered with hanging beads. Nick glanced down to his chest and tucked the leather thong inside his shirt.

As Vicente came through the beaded doorway smiling, Nick noticed that his mustache had grown out well already. The Mexican grasped Nick's hand in both of his.

"Good to see you, Nicholas. How are you enjoying your vacation?"

Vicente's English was good but Nick thought he did not say "vacation" quite right. The pronunciation was fine but there was something wrong with the emphasis.

"I am relaxing."

"Good. Did you go to the cemetery today to see our celebration of death?"

"Yes. It's like nothing else I've seen."

"Most Americans find The Day of the Dead distasteful. But for us, to be reminded of the nearness of death makes life seem more valuable."

Nick said, "It's a good celebration. It makes death a part of life—which of course it is."

"Exactly!"

Nick looked into the glass display cases at the weathered figurines and pottery arranged there. "It all looks very old and authentic to me. How can one tell what's fake?"

Vicente smiled, took a key ring from his pocket, and unlocked the case in front of him. He reached in to retrieve a faded clay vase with a tableau of birds, men, and maize etched below its neck.

"This material, for example, is very, very old. Older than one can imagine. But until a few weeks ago it was just a lump of clay."

He handed it to Nick and continued:

"That's part of the difficulty in authenticating pieces. We are not manufacturing materials, just reshaping nature a bit. But as a practical matter you can be assured that my total collection consists only of recreations. The Mexican government—on behalf of the people—claims ownership of all antiquities. Dealing in them is not permitted."

"But some people believe. . ."

"What they want to believe. I cannot protect people from themselves."

Nick turned the vase upside-down.

"You could stamp 'Hecho en México' into the bottom of each piece."

Vicente shrugged. "We all have to make a living. As soon as I do that I am no longer in the art business but the souvenir business."

"But if the experts can't tell what's real and it's illegal to take art treasures out of Mexico, how can you get your works through customs?"

Vicente frowned and reached to take the vase from Nick.

"These days the federales are looking for drugs, not old Olmec bowls. And besides. . ."

As the clay piece passed between them Vicente juggled it and it fell to the stone floor, cracking with a pop into a dozen large pieces, a hundred small fragments, and a thousand grains of powder.

Nick stepped back. "I'm sorry. I thought you had it."

Vicente stooped, picked through the debris, and stood clutching a shard from the base of the jug between thumb and forefinger. He held it up to Nick.

"Here is your proof. Here is my insurance against the federales."

Nick took the fragment from Vicente and frowned at it. Embedded in the clay was a peso coin dated 1971.

"That has saved me a night in jail more than once."

Nick nodded as though impressed. But how many pieces would you have to break to find the one without the coin?

Vicente went on:

"But now my life is not so exciting. The business has grown and I am tied to my shop and fábrica. The federales know my label and I just ship my orders to galleries in the States." He nodded toward a crate of pottery against the wall ready to be sealed. "It has become very routine."

Nick moved to the crate and lifted a vase from it. He examined it as Vicente eyed him closely.

The Mexican said, "Is there anything else that interests you? Perhaps something less fragile to take back home with you. Something in stone or jade perhaps?"

Nick bent to replace the vase in the crate and killed an urge to make sure the amulet was still tucked inside his shirt. He straightened up.

"I'm not a collector. But I have friends in the States who might be interested. I still have your card."

Vicente turned his back to Nick and took something from a glass case on the wall.

"I wish to present you with a gift so you might begin to become a collector. Please. I want you to have it."

When Vicente turned back and held out his hand, in his palm sat a polished death's head cut from black stone.

"Miquitzli," Nick whispered reflexively, and wished immediately he hadn't said it. Too much death for one day—it was getting to him. He did not look up but felt Vicente's eyes boring into him.

He walked through desert countryside. No trees, only dried bushes that looked like withered hands; hard earth half soil, half sand. The sun sat straight overhead. No breeze, no sound.

As he walked, the ground in front of him began to move as though someone trapped beneath the desert floor was trying to escape. Nick dropped to his knees and began digging at the brittle earth with his fingers.

Then somehow it changed—and Nick found himself buried beneath the sand, struggling to escape the isolated grave. He could barely breathe in the arid darkness and clawed frantically, but the sand kept pouring in on him.

He heard a crack, then a flash of lightning came through the opening in the stone wall above his bed and he saw that he had thrown the gray Indian blanket to the floor of his room.

The dark clouds he had first seen as he left Malena's house had found Escondido. Rain pelted the shutters and beat hard on the roof. As more lightning boomed and cracked like artillery fire Nick moved from the bed to the desk and flipped on the lamp. But as the electric bulb lit the room, he jerked his hand back from a black shape on the desk. Then he saw it was only the death's head Vicente had given him. Still, he lifted it from the desk and placed it in the bottom of his suitcase, out of sight. Nick went back to bed with the light burning and eyes open, wishing Malena were there to comfort him and dispel the nightmare terror that still haunted him.

Something had happened between them that he could not very well explain. It was nothing like what he once had with his wife: They had shared a cynical view of the world; she was beautiful and formidable and he loved her for it.

But this was different. Seemingly he had little in common with Malena. Yet something about her ground around irrationally inside his chest and in the pit of his stomach when they were apart—a palpable longing, as if she had bewitched him. And now he was alone and still jumping when the artillery fired, wishing she were there with him. It was then he heard a pounding at the door.

Nick hesitated only an instant. He went to the door and pulled it open without first calling out to ask who it might be. Malena was standing in the dark rain as he knew she would be, water beading on her face, staring at him with wide eyes. He pulled her inside.

Nick tore open the buttons of her sodden dress and slid it off her shoulders. She stood naked and shivering with arms held at her sides, her flesh tight from the cold water. He took the blanket from where he had thrown it on the floor and wrapped her in it. From the shower he retrieved a towel, and Malena sat at the desk pressing her straight black hair in it while Nick built a fire in the chimenea. Still neither said a word.

When the fire was going he poured two brandies. She sat on the floor in front of the fireplace with the blanket wrapped around her. Nick handed her a brandy and sat beside her. After they had both drunk from their glasses she turned to him and finally spoke:

"I heard you call. You knew I would come."

He lit a cigarette and stared into the fire biting his bottom lip. This was not why he had come to Mexico. He had come only to settle things with his father. This was nothing he wanted nor understood.

She went on: "I know what people say about me. That I am a witch, because I can see things that they cannot. . .And now I know you are the same."

A spark leapt from the fire with a crack and Nick started. Malena stroked her hand over his chest.

"Tranquilo, guapito." She looked at him with dark eyes that seemed even deeper with the red flames reflecting in them. "No te preocupes. Do not worry. It is not bad to be thus. It is only that we are special."

■

Nick came through the front door of the apartment gym bag in hand, dropped it to the floor, and hung his letter jacket on the peg in the vestibule. Seeing his father sitting in his easy chair smoking his pipe and reading a thick book by late afternoon light slanting through the venetian blinds, he called, "We won. Twenty-seven thirteen."

His father looked up at him standing beneath the arched portal between the vestibule and living room and frowned.

"What happened to your head?"

Nick paused a beat. Then he remembered and reached up reflexively to the bandage above his right eye.

"Oh, that. I must've gotten kicked or something."

"There are other uses for your head. That is, if you haven't had your good sense kicked out of it already."

Nick took a deep breath. "This is what I want to do. You forget what it's like to be my age."

"No, I remember very clearly. I recall sitting up late at night studying Greek and Latin for my entrance exams."

Nick shook his head. "This isn't the old country, Dad. I don't need all that. Americans do things. They don't sit around thinking."

"That I cannot argue with. But, yes, here you can do whatever you want— including read whatever you want, pursue whatever work you want, go to any university. You have the intellect, Nicholas, but for some reason you prefer to run around in yellow pants knocking people down."

Nick took a step forward into the living room. "You went to my game?"

His father gave a flip of his hand that both admitted and at the same time dismissed his attendance.

"This is foolishness, Nicholas, an illusion. A waste of your time and your talents and a good chance to cripple yourself. . .You'll learn that there are deeper, more satisfying pleasures in life. Yes, I can see that you earn the adulation of your peers and a certain status. But what will you have in two years when it's time to go to university? An empty head, which the crackpots will love to fill with their theories."

"No, I already have yours."

Nick was sorry he'd said it as soon as it left his lips and hung his head as if to deflect his father's gaze. Long seconds passed.

Then finally his father said, "Yes, it seems you are a typical American. Forgive me for ever suggesting you might somehow be special."

And he went back to his book.

Seven

Nick rolled over in bed and reached out to put his arm around Malena but she was gone. He opened his eyes to bright, mid-morning light and saw a silhouette standing at the foot of the bed—the silhouette of a man. Nick sat up straight with his heart racing.

He squinted and as his eyes adjusted to the light saw that it was Francisco, who stood with arms hanging limp at his sides, face expressionless.

"Francisco! Qué pasa?"

The Mexican, who normally spoke a nasal, singsong Spanish, said in a flat, monotone voice, "I do not wish to ask this of you but there is no one else. Those who are willing are not able and those who are able—like my boss, the cabrón who owns the taxi—are not willing, so..."

"What is it?" Nick swung his legs over the side of the bed and pulled on his trousers. "What do you need?"

"The hospital will not give me the body of my wife until I pay the bill and..."

"Barbarita...?"

"She is dead."

Nick pulled the chair out from the desk. "Siéntese."

Francisco perched on the edge of the chair. Nick washed a glass in the basin, poured a brandy, and carried it to him. Then he opened the shutters behind him.

"I will do whatever I can to help but tell me. . ."

"It is much money. I will repay you."

"What happened, Pancho?"

"We have to bury her tomorrow. It is the law. I did not know the hospital would be so expensive. I did not think about how much it would cost. I thought I could pay little by little. . ."

He told Nick what he needed—it was a lot of money, at least for Francisco. Nick nodded.

"No hay problema. You will have the money."

Through the open window Nick saw Andrés passing with a tray and called to him, "Andrés! Por favor, bring us some coffee and two cups."

Andrés nodded and disappeared down the stairs. When Nick turned back, Francisco was sipping from the brandy.

"Gracias, amigo," he said blowing out a long breath and letting his shoulders drop.

Soon Andrés came with the coffee and cups on a tray that he passed through the window. Nick set the tray on the desk.

"You told me she was not well but also that the doctor wasn't worried."

"It happened very quickly. I have not slept for two nights. . ."

Nick handed him a cup and sat on the end of the bed.

". . .We did not know she was pregnant. Then it happened. The child aborted himself. The blood came and would not stop.

"I took her to Dr. Sanchez. He had to operate to stop the flow. Which he did and said she would be well soon."

He looked up from his cup. "That is when I saw you—Monday."

Nick nodded.

"But then there was fever, an infection.

"The ambulance took her to the hospital in Santa Cruz—fifty

kilometers from here more or less. They have a machine there for the kidneys. The infection had spread."

Nick felt his stomach rising and the coffee did not help.

"They tried for two days but nothing could save her."

Francisco sipped his coffee and stared blankly at the cup. "It is God's will."

Through the open window behind Francisco Nick could see a blue sky and cotton-like clouds. Another beautiful day. Then he, too, sipped his coffee and stared into the cup.

When they stepped from the hotel, Martín was waiting in the street beside his pickup truck. He shook Nick's hand, slid into the cab, and started the engine. Francisco and Nick climbed in beside him.

At the bank the two brothers waited in the truck. Nick signed over traveler's checks and got cash. Outside he handed it to Francisco, who took the money without looking at it and buttoned it away in his shirt pocket.

Martín moved the truck over rough, cobbled streets. No one said anything. Soon the pickup stopped at a carpenter's shop with pine coffins stacked inside. As Francisco went in, Martín turned to Nick.

"Gracias a Dios that you were here and ready to help, for one must properly bury one's dead and there was no one else. Don Vicente had refused to loan Pancho the money and take it from his pay."

"Don Vicente?"

"Sí. He owns the taxi Pancho drives."

Martín looked ahead through the windshield at nothing in particular. "I don't want to think about what the hospital would have done with Barbarita's body if we could not pay the bill. Nor do I want to think about what Pancho would have done to get the money."

The fifty kilometer drive to the hospital in Santa Cruz seemed interminable to Nick. The road was so filled with ruts and potholes that at times the truck barely moved, and neither Martín nor Francisco spoke a word. Also, the pickup followed the hearse carrying Barbarita's coffin, visible through its back window, so the three men stared silently at the pine coffin the entire drive, which seemed never-ending.

The hospital, a new one-story structure near the town center, looked as if its funding had run out before it could be finished. Upon entering, Nick noticed patches of missing mosaic, scaffolding in a yet-to-be-painted hallway, bed sheets draped over passages where doors still had to be hung. The waiting room had no chairs, only a wooden bench built into the stucco wall. On the bench sat a dark-skinned old Indian woman wearing a black shawl. Francisco went up to her, kissed her cheek, and put his arm around her.

"Now you can go home, Mamá."

"You have the money?"

"Sí. I will pay the bill."

"Gracias a Dios. Now we can go."

Francisco moved to the reception desk in the lobby, unfolded the bills from his shirt pocket, and began counting them out aloud, one-by-one, as a young woman in white behind the desk counted along silently.

Martín came up behind Nick shaking his head.

"For two days our mother has kept a vigil. We brought her food and she slept sitting on the wooden bench."

"But Barbarita died last night, didn't she?"

"Sí. But my mother is the daughter of slaves. She would not leave even after Barbarita died for fear they would arrest her for running out on the bill."

"Nicholas. . ."

Nick turned and saw Francisco waving him over.

"Count this again, hombre. See if it is right."

The girl behind the reception now fixed her eyes on Nick as he studied the bill for services, re-added the figures in his head, and recounted the money. Business first, last, always. Then he handed the wad to Francisco, who handed it to the girl. She took it, locked it away in the desk, then pointed to a frosted glass door across the lobby.

"Allí." That was all she said: There.

Francisco crossed the lobby to the glass door, his jaw set. At the door he paused, then reached for the handle and pushed it open.

From behind, Nick saw sunlight coming through a window high in the wall and falling on a metal cart. On the cart, under a rumpled white sheet splotched reddish-brown, lay a body. Francisco reached up and folded back the sheet from her face.

From where Nick stood at the reception desk Barbarita seemed a handsome young woman. Smooth dark skin, round-faced, perhaps twenty-five—as old as she would get. Francisco's mother stepped into the room with him, closing the glass door behind her.

The two men from the hearse came into the lobby. Nick nodded and offered cigarettes. Nick, Martín, and the men from the hearse smoked silently, avoiding each other's eyes, conscious of the muffled prayers coming through the glass door. Suddenly Nick felt that he was being watched and looked up to find the girl at the reception staring at him. When he returned her gaze she dropped her head and got busy with something on the desk.

The click of the latch on the glass door made all four men turn there in unison. Francisco came out with his mother. The two men from the hearse crushed out their cigarettes on the stone floor and went in. After a few seconds they came out pushing the metal cart with

Barbarita on it and led a procession through hallways smelling of fresh paint, out the back door of the hospital, and into a bare earth plaza hidden behind high concrete walls, empty except for an incinerator, garbage cans, and the hearse, which had been backed through wooden gates. The sun beat down on Barbarita's wooden coffin awaiting her on a gurney. The men wheeled the cart beside it, turned, and lifted their chins toward Martín and Nick.

Martín moved to the cart, pulled back the blood-splattered hospital sheet, and tossed it to the ground. As Nick approached he saw that Barbarita wore a pale green nightgown, it also spotted with dried blood. The aroma of alcohol rose to him.

Martín put his hands under her shoulders, the hearse drivers slid their arms beneath the body, and Nick grabbed her ankles, surprised to find how cold her flesh felt. As the four men lifted her into the coffin Nick noticed a small mirror that had been attached inside the coffin lid, directly over her face. He looked from the mirror to Barbarita's face and shivered.

Francisco moved forward to the coffin. He touched Barbarita's cold hand, then her face, and collapsed across her, wailing a wild, primitive call that made Nick think of a lone pariah baying in the dark.

Martín moved behind his brother and pulled him upright. Francisco gripped the edge of the casket, threw back his head, and howled a piercing cry that echoed off the concrete walls. Nick moved around the incinerator to the other side of the plaza, but there was no escaping the sound.

When Francisco finally turned away from Barbarita the drivers hurriedly closed the lid of the coffin and wheeled the gurney into the hearse. Francisco's mother sat in the hearse by her son's dead wife. Martín told the driver to go on ahead.

Francisco, Martín, and Nick walked back through the hospital, past the reception where the young woman in white stared at them stupidly, and out the front door to the street. There Martín pointed to a white wooden cart at the corner where a vendor was cutting blood-red watermelon.

"Sandía?"

Francisco nodded.

The three men leaned into the shade of an old, flaking, three-story building, using toothpicks to spear the red flesh of the melon from plastic cups. The sweet, clean flavor of the fruit settled on Nick but failed to cleanse from his mouth the taste of death. Then he felt Francisco elbowing him.

"Look, Nicholas."

He looked up. Across the street on the opposite sidewalk a man pushed himself along on the base of a sawed-off shopping cart. The man, too, seemed to have been sawn in half, shorn at the waist.

Francisco shook his head.

"Qué hombre! Where did he get that cart? There's no supermarket within a hundred kilometers."

Nick looked at Francisco then back to his resourceful countryman pushing himself down the sidewalk as best he could.

Nick sat watching the turning blades of the cantina's ceiling fan. They seemed to swat at the air, miss, and squawk quietly, stirring no breeze. When the bartender looked up from his newspaper Nick lifted his chin toward the brown bottle on the table in front of him.

He lit another cigarette as the man brought another beer and took away the empty. Maybe this one would wash away the dusty taste of the plaza behind the hospital. He had already washed his hands.

The turning fan blades carried him back to a similar place. A worn foot rail at the bar, rank spittoons with floating cigar butts, a half-naked woman pictured on an out-dated calendar, and a ceiling fan rotating slowly but doing no apparent good. The electric bulbs were dark so as not to add to the heat of the day, the only light coming through half-painted windows and an open door. There had even been a cobblestone street. His father walked to the university or rode the streetcar when it rained. Nicholas would wait for him on the corner, and his father would take him into the tavern, where the son would drink a root beer because it came in a brown bottle like his father's bock. . .It all seemed further in the past than it actually was, in part because so much changed. The spittoons and girly calendar had been removed, the cobblestones and streetcar tracks covered with asphalt, the front door of the tavern closed with air conditioner humming. The last time he had gone there with his father for a beer he had felt claustrophobic, closed in by dark windows and the sealed door.

Now two dark, faceless figures came through the swinging half-doors and stood silhouetted in the sunlight behind them. But Nick recognized the tall, thin outline and the squat, square one beside it, each crowned with the sloping cap of the Mexican Army. They moved straight for Nick and he saw that Raúl was grinning, fat and unctuous. Jaime moved his mustache just a bit in the direction of a smile.

"Buenas tardes."

"Como estás?"

"How good to see you."

The usual handshaking and insincerities.

"I was just saying to Jaime, 'Where is our yellow-haired friend? We have not seen him for a week.' And there you are, sitting in a cool cantina, drinking a beer, enjoying your vacation."

And here I am, thought Nick, enjoying myself.

"But for us it is all work, day and night. No time to rest."

"But surely you have time for a beer," Nick said. "I wish to invite you." Yet another insincerity.

Raúl scratched his chest and looked at Jaime with raised eyebrows as though trying to decide.

They pulled up chairs and Nick motioned to the bartender to bring over a round. Raúl lifted his cap, wiped perspiration from his forehead with his sleeve, and tossed the cap on the table.

"What a day! What a night!"

The beer came and then the saludes and the knocking together of bottles, and Nick thought of the tavern downstairs and the manly scent of his father and how good it had all once seemed.

They drank from the bottles. Raúl took a handkerchief from his tunic pocket and sopped more sweat from his face.

"I hope your morning, Señor Nicholas, was more pleasant than ours."

Nick thought of his waking with Francisco standing at the foot of the bed and the ride to Santa Cruz behind the hearse. "Have you had problems?"

"Being a soldier is a job like any other. When people cooperate and everyone works together, everyone is happy. But when someone has a mind of his own, there are problems."

Both soldiers shook their heads and sighed as if to say, Why can't everyone just be happy? Raúl leaned across the table toward Nick.

"Last night we set up a roadblock. It's like fishing with a net. You never know what you might catch.

"At midnight we netted a little fish—a little fish from your country. But he could lead us to the big fish. So we take him to the church and we ask him:

"'Where did you buy the heroin?'

"'To whom are you to deliver it in the United States?'

"'Who gave you the money to buy it?'

"He seemed like a nice young man. Like you: yellow hair, blue eyes. From Wisconsin his card says."

Nick nodded. Wheeze cone scene. Raúl continued:

"A nice young man perhaps. But he will not cooperate. He wants to make problems. We do not want problems, but. . ." Raúl shrugged and looked to Jaime, who shook his head in agreement.

Nick signaled the bartender for three more. Raúl waited for the beer to arrive. When the bartender was out of earshot he went on in a bored, singsong voice.

"We put him on the table, his head hanging over the edge, back like this. . .I hold my hand over his mouth, shake the bottle of mineral water, and—tzip!—shoot the Tehuacan up his nose.

"We ask again, 'Where did you buy it, where will you take it, who gave you the money?'. . .But no cooperation. None.

"So we turn him on his stomach, pull up his shirt, and, with the pistol flat. . ."

Raúl brought his palm down on the table with a slap, making Nick start.

". . .on the kidneys. And again. But still he would not help us."

The two soldiers moved their heads from side to side in rhythm with the slicing fan blades. Nick sipped at his beer, but it tasted like bile and did not seem to reach his stomach.

"Well. So now we turn him over on his back, take down his pantalones, and tie him spread to the table. We plug the electric cord into the wall, touch the wires to his huevos just for a little moment, and wait for a change of heart. Then again. . .But not too much."

Jaime must have thought that point needed elaboration, or had perceived a blank look in Nick's eyes that he misread as a lack of comprehension, for he slid his right hand between the buttons of his olive tunic and patted his chest with short, rapid strokes.

"El corazón," he said. Then he made a gesture with his hands like an umpire calling a man safe at the plate but that meant just the opposite. "Como el otro."

Raúl took a drink, wiped his mouth with his hand, and leaned back in his chair, blowing out a slow breath.

"A long, difficult night. Only just now has the young American told us what he could have told us hours ago. He had to tell us eventually, so why make problems?"

Jaime pursed his lips and shook his head as though wondering why some people just insisted on making problems. The cantina sat silent except for the faint, repetitive squeaking of the ceiling fan turning above them.

Under different circumstances Nick's thoughts and sympathies might have been with his countryman around the corner in the back of the church, the confessed drug-runner with testicles burnt raw, an aching back, and a stomach that likely had been turning inside-out so long that vomiting now served no useful purpose. But Nick gave the failed adventurer from Wisconsin hardly a passing thought. Rather, his mind had fixed on the one thing that Jaime had said—"the heart"—and on his spare gesture that showed how it might stop beating. For that was what the autopsy report—signed by Dr. E. E. Sanchez and sent from the United States Embassy in Mexico City—had said: That the heart had stopped. Even though he had never before had heart problems, had lived a vigorous life of moderation, had been told by his doctor that he'd live to be one hundred, but was now dead at sixty-six.

"The heart," Jaime had said. "Como el otro." Like the other. Like the other gringo whose heart had failed when they overdid it just a bit with the wires. A man who made problems by refusing to cooperate because he knew nothing. A man who somehow got caught in a net meant for more predatory fish.

No, Nick did not really give a damn about the asshole from Wisconsin who had fucked up, but thought more on the possibility that he was drinking with his father's executioners—though it was no doubt a case of mistaken identity or the like. Jaime and Raúl were well-meaning (though perhaps a bit overzealous) and doing a very difficult job—and certainly didn't intend for that to happen. But then, of course, the old man would not cooperate.

Nick looked at the two dark, smiling soldiers sitting in the dim, late afternoon light. He could think of nothing to say to his drinking companions in response to their admirable frankness and bonhomie, to their sharing of their day's problems. So the three of them sat smiling at each other in the cool, shadowy quiet of the cantina listening to the fan squeak.

■

"No, Nicholas. I absolutely forbid it."

"I'm eighteen. You can't stop me."

His father looked up from his dinner plate, set down his knife and fork, and stared at Nick as though he had discovered a stranger sitting across the dinner table from him. Finally he said, "You will obey me."

Nick swallowed down the lump in his throat and felt welling in his eyes hot tears, which he fought to suppress.

"I have to go."

"If you must go somewhere go to university. You won't have to fight."

"I'm no draft-dodger," Nick shot back, sensing that his voice was near cracking.

His father shook his head as though in disgust.

"Your mother's grandfather refused to fight the French and supported the Commune. My father left Silesia to avoid Prussian conscription. Your mother and I fled Poland at the last war. Now you choose to travel to the other side of the world to oppress complete strangers. It is too much."

Nick's father threw his napkin on his plate, pushed up from the table, and paced across the polished floor. At the faux fireplace he stopped and took a Mayan stone figurine from the mantel, turning it in his hand as if appraising it.

"Nations come and go. Civilizations flourish then suddenly disappear." *He turned to face his son. "How many men gave their lives extending the Mayan Empire? How many died building the pyramids at Teotihuacan? Of*

what value is their sacrifice now?

"History happens no matter what you or I do. Don't throw your life away, Nicholas."

Now Nick saw his father halt momentarily, as if he had heard a distant sound. His eyes grew suddenly glassy; his bottom lip trembled for just an instant.

"Maria, if she were alive, would never let her son go to war. She would have taken you to Canada or chained herself to you to keep you from leaving…I would betray her memory by allowing you to go. So I must say 'no'."

As his father resumed his place at the table Nick took a deep breath.

"I'm going."

"I say you cannot and that is all I will say on the matter. Now will you obey your father?"

Nick felt his stomach turning queasily, felt his mouth go suddenly dry.

"Not this time. No."

His father glared at him as though in shock, looking Nick up and down.

"'No' what?"

Nick dropped his gaze to his dinner plate. "No, sir."

Professor Petrov once again placed his napkin on his lap and retrieved his knife and fork. As he chewed he gestured with his knife, cutting at the air with a backhand swipe, as if chasing away a bothersome fly.

"There is no honor in death, Nicholas. None whatsoever. I pray you live long enough to learn that lesson."

Eight

No, the stomach did not feel good and his legs wobbled as he moved down the hill toward the zócalo. What did he have to eat all day? Nothing, he remembered, but the watermelon from the vendor near the hospital. Now it was late afternoon, he'd had five—or was it six?—Victorias at the cantina, and his stomach kept growling.

The walk up the hill and down again wasn't doing him any good either. He'd found Dr. Sanchez's surgery near the crest, enclosed within a high, rose-colored wall behind which Nick could see the second floor of the physician's house and the tops of tall palms. But, outside, a line of stoic mestizos stood against the wall waiting to see the doctor. So Nick turned around and came back down the hill, the stomach feeling worse than ever, his knees shaky from the climb, and the bad ankle hurting where the screws held it together.

At the zócalo the grackles in the elms cackled annoyingly as he strode across the square and moved through the hotel portal. Nick veered to the left and crossed the courtyard toward the kitchen, where the women cooked very good chiles in cream, chicken with rice, and green stews. But as Nick moved from bright sunlight into shade he ran right up to the table where Don Vicente and his two men were finishing their comida with coffee and brandy.

"Ah, Nicholas. Have a drink with us. Are you still drinking beer? Andrés!"

Nick had already had more than enough to drink and all he

wanted was some ballast for his stomach. Besides, of what further use was Vicente? At first Nick had thought Vicente might know something that would help explain his father's death, since the antiquities he dealt were likely what brought his father to Escondido. But now there was no reason to drink with the rich cabrón who refused Francisco the money to bury his wife.

But the alcohol had slowed Nick's brain and his tongue. He hesitated too long and found himself nodding and sliding into a chair across the table from Vicente.

A brown bottle was placed in front of him and he drank, but the beer seemed soured. He heard Vicente ask, "And how are you enjoying your vacation?"

Nick drank the beer and ordered pollo en adobo. By the time the food arrived he had drunk another and then, since he was headed in that direction anyway, had one with dinner. Afterward, Vicente poured him a brandy to go with his coffee and flan and kept filling the glass whenever he could. Vicente and his two men kept pace and by sunset were glassy, too, but not nearly as bad as Nick.

Liquor, he noted, was infinitely more subtle than electricity, but it was an interrogation nonetheless. However, Nick figured Vicente had every reason to be wary of him if Vicente was, in fact, illegally dealing in protected artifacts. Nick's presence in Escondido didn't fit.

"You seem to know more about our mythology than you first let on, Nicholas," Vicente said.

"What do you mean?"

But Nick knew exactly what he meant. He knew at the time that it had been a mistake—no wonder Vicente was suspicious.

"Yesterday in my shop when I handed you the Deity of Death you muttered, 'Miquitzli', as though you were well acquainted with him."

"I've been reading up on it. Andrés gave me some English-language books to help me pass the time. There was a good one on pre-Columbian mythology."

He saw Vicente thinking and figured he would ask Andrés later. Vicente tried another tack.

"I see you have met the witch Malena."

Nick said nothing.

"To travel and meet new people—very seductive the strangeness of a different culture. It can be very exciting for a while, very refreshing to have such an affair."

"What affair are you talking about?"

"Forgive me. It is none of my business."

Nick did not disagree.

Finally, Vicente put his elbows on the table and folded his hands near Nick's. He glanced at Luis and Miguel, who excused themselves and stood. When they were gone Vicente said, "I know you are here for a reason, Nicholas. Perhaps I can help you. Little of importance occurs in Escondido that I am not aware of—particularly anything of a commercial nature. If there is something you need, something you wish to buy, I would like to help."

Nick could feel his brain sloshing inside his skull and knew he would soon be sick.

"Yes, there is something. . ."

Vicente leaned even closer.

"My tourist card expires soon. I was given only a thirty-day visa. I understand one can have this taken care of for a price."

Vicente glared and Nick saw that his eyes were focused on his chest. He reached down and tucked the jade Kukulcan back inside his shirt.

Vicente said, "There I cannot help you."

Nick managed to stagger upstairs, burst through the door to his room, and lurch to the toilet before he threw up.

Certainly he had drunk too much on a near-empty stomach. Or it might have been something he had eaten. Or too much hot sun, or too much the feel of Barbarita's cold legs. Or perhaps too much new knowledge to digest—the knowledge that his father's last moments had likely been spent at the Church of the Inquisition in the hands of Raúl and Jaime. For whatever reasons, he was sick. Then he stood under the cold shower as if trying to wash the day away before collapsing face down on the bed.

It was dark and quiet when he awoke and he had no idea where he was. Yes, Mexico. Nighttime apparently. Nick rose unsteadily from the bed. He had fallen across it diagonally and lain for hours on his stomach with his feet hanging over the side, and now his back hurt. He groped for the lamp on the desk, found it, and squinted hard against the light.

A sharp pain zigzagged between his eyes. Nick poured water into a glass from the terracotta pitcher on the desk, drank it off, and poured another. He looked at his watch. Nearly midnight. And now with a bilious taste from his stomach it all came back to him.

Again he stood under the shower, running cold water on the back of his neck. Midnight was a hell of a time to wake up. He turned the faucet off and grabbed the towel from a nail driven into the concrete wall. He pulled on his jeans and shirt and soon was stepping through the hotel portal to the street.

The stars looked cold and dark. Everything seemed to have dimmed and weakened and become less vivid than it had been. He felt no passion for anything. He felt nothing for nothing.

Near the market he saw a light inside a shop that sold beer, refrescos, and canned goods to farmers who arrived in town at all hours. The old woman behind the splintered counter handed Nick two aspirins sealed in cellophane and opened the bottle of mineral water he pulled from the cooler. Across the street on the loading dock of the market Nick saw men curled around each other like sleeping dogs, their straw sombreros covering their eyes. Pariahs sniffed at the garbage in the street and somewhere a radio played mariachi music. He washed down the aspirins with the mineral water and moved down the hill away from the center of town.

At Malena's casita he knocked and waited. Then he beat on the door with his fist, put an ear to it, and cupped his hands around his mouth to call through it, "Malena. . .Malena! Soy yo. It's me."

Finally he turned and moved back up the hill.

Nick picked his way through a labyrinth of quiet, black alleyways and soon found himself on the street where light and music poured from the open door. He moved to the light, stepped up on the sidewalk, and paused.

A large and noisy crowd filled La Última Cena. Standing in the doorway gazing down into the cellar, moving his eyes back and forth over the dance floor, Nick finally spotted her. There. In a white cotton dress lying open at the neck, draping from her square shoulders, making her skin look even more brown. The dress hung smooth on her hips, suggesting the shape of her buttocks, and his thoughts returned momentarily to the previous afternoon in bed with her.

As he moved down the steps into the tavern, the music surrounded him. But he chose not to cross the room to her, instead leaning into the shadow of a stone pillar in the dark cellar and watching her from afar.

Again she danced alone. When she bent forward or moved her

head from side to side the black hair fell across her face and onto the white shoulders of the dress. He remembered her kneeling naked over him and the black hair and brown body against his light bronze skin and the translucent hair on his chest.

Nick heard loud voices coming from the bar and turned. There Vicente gestured to the barman and pointed to a table of young couples where he apparently wanted drinks delivered. Red-eyed and disheveled, Vicente looked as if he had been at it since Nick left him in the restaurant at dusk. Luis and Miguel, his seeming bodyguards, also stood at the bar, as always tan, handsome, inseparable. Tight pants, loose silk shirts, togetherness.

Nick looked back to Malena moving smoothly to the salsa, dancing with no one and everyone, just as he had first encountered her. He now saw her look up—not at him this time but at Don Vicente.

Vicente had moved onto the dance floor and was crossing toward her in front of the band and attempting a suave smile that seemed more a lecherous grin. She watched his approach but did not return his smile. As he began to dance arrhythmically in front of her she turned her head away, continuing to dance as before, as if alone.

Vicente leaned forward to whisper in her ear and teetered. Malena backed away. Vicente stumbled forward, his lips moving. When she shook her head 'no' he reached his arms around her waist and pulled her toward him, sliding his hands down to her hips and pressing his groin against hers. At the bar Luis and Miguel laughed as Malena tried to push him away.

Nick found himself striding across the floor of the tavern. It seemed to take him no time at all to get to the dance floor, push his way through the dancers, and reach out for Vicente. But then everything slowed.

He grabbed Vicente's arm. . .Vicente spun around, eyes opened wide. . .Nick saw him pull back his arm as if to strike then watched his own fist plunge into Vicente's Adam's apple. . .The heavy man reeled backwards toward the band. . .Nick heard a scream and turned to see a look of horror in Malena's eyes. . .He felt a dull jolt in the back of his skull, then everything began turning and going dark. . .

When he came to, the first thing he sensed was that the band had stopped playing. Then he heard Malena's voice in his ear:

"Nicholas. . .Nicholas. . ."

He felt moisture on the back of his neck and realized she was cradling his head in her arms. He opened his eyes.

A crowd of patrons encircled him but no one was getting too close. They looked at him askance, as though to avoid the appearance of direct sympathy. The dizziness lessened and he sat up with Malena's help.

"Estoy bien—I'm okay," he said but knew from the look on her face that she did not believe him.

"Can you walk?" she asked.

"I think so."

"Vámonos. Before the police arrive."

Nick got to his feet with Malena steadying him, but then staggered and spun toward the bandstand. The bass player looked down at him warily and then to Vicente standing nearby. Surrounded by a group of men, his eyes red and watery, Vicente smiled at Nick a feline smile that was all mouth and no eyes. Malena grabbed Nick and steered him toward the door.

The crowd parted, making an aisle to the doorway as the band began again to play. Nick thought of a wedding march. The bride in her white dress (now stained with blood), clutching tight the groom's arm (to keep him from falling), the two of them rushing off together (not to honeymoon but to escape the police). And, instead of being showered by ritual rice, one of Vicente's two men, who was standing at the door, spit on Nick's neck as they passed.

Nick whirled, but Malena tugged roughly on his sleeve, tearing his shirt at the shoulder and pulling him out onto the sidewalk. A pulsing red light reflected down the street to their left; they moved off to the right arm-in-arm and were soon at the end of the block and safely around the corner.

At the street where they should have turned for Malena's casita they continued walking straight, moving up the hill. He looked at her. "A dónde vamos?"

"To the doctor. The cut from the bottle needs to be sewn."

"A bottle? Who hit me?"

"One of the two. Not the one at the door, the other."

"Then what happened?"

"Don't think about it now."

"Tell me. I wish to know."

"It's not important. There wasn't much more. The one with the bottle tried to kick you, but I pushed him away and knelt over you. He knew if he touched me the others would kill him."

"Gracias."

"Al contrario. My thanks to you. But. . ."

"But what, Malena?"

"I am afraid for us."

"Don't worry. Your gods and white magic will protect us," he said, surprised at his own optimistic-sounding words and wondering whether perhaps he really meant it.

She wrapped her arms around his waist and they moved in step up the hill to the high side of town and the doctor's house.

The stars shone brightly. The night—quiet, still, and warm— seemed suddenly peaceful. He kissed Malena's hair as they walked and felt her arms tighten around him. But then they both stopped dead as a loud howling broke forth from the dark street in front of them.

They moved forward tentatively then saw the animal, a large, hungry-looking cur with matted gray hair that made it appear part wolf. It sat outside an iron gate making an eerie, wolf-like cry. Inside the gate within the walls of a flowered patio a well-groomed German shepherd cowered. It peered at the gray dog and whimpered, bobbing its head from side to side.

Again the pariah on the outside bayed a wild, mournful cry that reminded Nick of Francisco's pained howling over Barbarita's body and made the skin on his arms crawl. He and Malena squeezed against the wall on the far side of the street and edged by, giving the animal as wide a berth as possible.

Half a block away Malena turned as they walked to look over her shoulder and let out a breath.

"These animals can be dangerous, particularly when they run in packs. But worse is the howling. At times it is so bad I cannot sleep and go outside to throw a stone at them. But they simply move beyond my range and continue to howl. I believe that they howl at all the fenced dogs, urging them to escape."

The howling grew fainter as they walked and Nick stopped to light a cigarette.

"Can't they catch these dogs and destroy them?"

As his match illuminated her face he saw her nodding. He had not smoked for years. Now the smoke smelled and tasted as it had when it all was new to him.

"Sí, sí. Each year the tame animals and the children are locked inside and men ride through the streets in the backs of trucks shooting the strays. They put the carcasses in the trucks and take them away."

"And then?"

"Then for a time it is quiet. But soon at night I will hear a howl, and the next night two."

They moved up the hill and stopped at a wrought-iron lamp on a rose-colored wall. Beneath the lamp was a door bell and a brass plate that read, "Dr. E. E. Sanchez, Medico Cirujano." Malena pressed the bell.

She waited a minute and pressed it again. Nick suddenly looked at her.

"Tell me, Malena. What was Vicente saying to you?"

"Tonterías. Nonsense."

"Such as?"

"It's not important."

"Yes, it is important."

She stared at him, thinking.

"He wants back the amulet I gave you."

That was probably true. Yet Nick figured it was only half the truth but left it alone.

Soon they heard quick footsteps and saw eyes behind a grate in the center of the door. The door opened a crack and an old man wearing a Jalisco-style sombrero stood staring at the blood smeared down the front of Malena's dress.

She said, "We wish to see Dr. Sanchez. The American gentleman is badly hurt."

The old man nodded rapidly and closed the door. They heard him scurrying away. Nick reached his hand up toward the back of his head but then decided he really didn't want to know and so did not touch it.

"It is bad, yes?"

"No. I only said so—and that you are a gringo—to give the doctor a reason to get out of bed. A campesino bleeding to death would have to wait till morning."

They heard the shuffling footsteps again and the door opened. The old man stood aside.

"Pase."

When Malena and Nick had stepped through the door the old man closed it behind them. They followed him through an open-air passageway filled with humid plants and smelling of earth and jasmine. Soon he led them into a brightly lit waiting room.

The white walls were ringed with dark, straight-back wooden chairs. Through an open door at the end of the room they saw a fiftyish man with salt-and-pepper goatee yawning and scratching his stomach. He wore bedroom slippers, a white pleated shirt, dark trousers. With a broad sweep of his arm he waved them into his surgery.

The doctor nodded toward an examination table with stirrups.

"Siéntese."

Nick sat and Malena paced back and forth. Dr. Sanchez washed his hands in a basin behind Nick and dried them on a hand towel. Nick spied a parchment from the University of Texas hanging on the wall in front of him.

Sanchez fingered the wound and asked, "Qué pasó?"

Nick took in a breath and opened his mouth to speak, but Malena broke in:

"Estabamos caminando. . .We were walking on a street where there are many old houses in disrepair. A brick fell from the wall and struck him."

As Sanchez looked at her with heavy eyelids Nick said in English, "I got hit with a bottle in a bar fight."

The doctor frowned at Nick, who lifted his chin toward the diploma on the wall, and the doctor's frown went away.

Sanchez took alcohol and cotton from a metal cabinet and began cleaning the wound.

"What was worth fighting for?"

"A woman."

Sanchez's eyes went to Malena for an instant. "American machismo. You'll need some stitches. Feel any nausea?"

Nick shook his head.

"Amnesia?"

"None that I recall."

Nick watched Malena. She listened carefully to the English but he wondered how much she understood.

Sanchez filled a syringe from a vial and made two injections near the gash in Nick's head. Then he took a needle and clear thread from the cabinet. He talked as he worked and Nick could smell a sweet, rancid cloud of whiskey coming from the doctor's stomach.

"I have not spoken English for a long time. Few North Americans come here."

"There are two others at the hotel now. And I know of another last month—the hotel loaned me books he left behind. They say he died suddenly."

"Ah, yes. I recall."

"You performed the autopsy?"

"I'm the only real doctor in town." He stopped for a moment and stared at Nick. The affable, blasé look had left the doctor's face. "Why do you want to know?"

The sudden silence made Malena stop her pacing. Her eyes moved back and forth between the two men. Nick turned his head to the side to return the doctor's stare.

"I'm curious how the man died."

Sanchez looked about the room as though hoping to discover an exit he hadn't been aware of.

"If you're from your government you already have the autopsy report. The man from the consulate came and verified the identity."

"I'm not from the government."

"Then what business is it of yours?"

Sanchez's face had turned red. Malena moved closer as if to intervene but a look from Nick stopped her. He said, "The dead man was my father."

Nick saw the blood drain from the doctor's face. Sanchez went back to work on Nick's scalp but more quickly now.

"I am very sorry for your father. I can see why you are curious. He seemed a healthy man in most regards but. . ."

Sanchez tied off the knot and snipped the thread with surgical scissors. He laid the bloodied needle on a table by the sink and spoke with his back to Nick as he washed his hands.

"But these things happen. Insufficient exercise, the unaccustomed altitude, and suddenly. . ."

"Shouldn't you have sterilized that needle?"

Sanchez turned with the towel in his hand.

"Don't worry. That was already taken care of."

Nick took the pack of Faros from his shirt pocket, lit one as he talked, and tried to appear calm.

"Later this morning Francisco Rosales will bury his wife, Barbara, at the panteón. Sunday you operated to stop her hemorrhaging; yesterday she died."

Sanchez focused on the hand towel. He straightened it, folded it, and laid it on the sink.

"I am sorry. There was nothing that could be done."

"Francisco believes Barbarita's death was the will of God. He knows nothing about sterilization and antibiotics. I hate to think what he would do if he came to believe his wife was taken from him by an unnecessary infection."

Sanchez stood with his arms folded in front of him. He opened his mouth to speak but nothing came out. Malena stared at Nick and folded her arms as well but as though suddenly chilled.

Finally Sanchez said, "She did not follow my instructions. You know how those people are."

Nick shook his head. "A woman should not have to die from that."

Sanchez turned away from Nick but did not argue. He made as if he was rearranging his surgical instruments that lay on the table. After a long moment he turned back and said, "There's nothing I can tell you about your father's death that you don't already know."

"You can tell me the truth."

"Truth? What is truth? This is Mexico not the United States. Your Anglo-Saxon logic does not apply. Much that occurs here is invisible; much that one sees is not real."

"Just tell me what you've seen. I'll figure out if it's real or not."

"And then what happens? I am in the middle."

Sanchez lowered himself onto a metal stool with rollers and stared at the tile floor. Nick felt his heart pumping in his chest.

"I do not want to cause problems for you. I'm concerned only with my father."

Nick's hands perspired, his head felt hot, and his ears hummed. He knew he could never tell Francisco something that would cause him more pain—that it was Sanchez, not God, who took Barbarita from him. When Sanchez sobered up and got hold of himself he'd probably figure that out. But then again he might never figure that a gringo would bother himself about "those people". Nick started in:

"Were there marks on the body—as if he'd been beaten or burnt or tortured?"

Sanchez looked up with raised eyebrows. "No. Nothing."

Nick glared at him.

"If you don't believe me ask your embassy. As always when an American dies alone they sent a consul to make the identity and order the autopsy. No, there was nothing like that."

"And the autopsy. What did that show?"

Sanchez's hands dangled in front of him. He examined his fingernails. "Nothing new."

"What do you mean 'nothing new'? What did you know?"

"I had learned that he died of a heart attack, that he had clutched his chest and collapsed. It was obvious."

"So you performed no thorough autopsy."

"There was no reason for a full autopsy."

"You were told that too?"

"They brought me the body and I did what I was asked to do. I met with the consul, put together an autopsy report, and embalmed the body. After a week when no one claimed it the corpse was buried."

Nick's head now felt very hot indeed and his ears rang but the room was still.

"So you know nothing except what the soldiers told you. That he had a heart attack."

Sanchez looked up with a deep furrow carved in his forehead. "Soldiers?"

"The drug soldiers who brought you the body."

Sanchez shook his head. "There were no soldiers. Only Vicente's men, Luis and Miguel."

Nick lay naked on the straw mat that served as Malena's bed. The ringing in his ears had intensified as had the feeling of heat, and now his skull was ringed with pulsing pain, as though in the jaws of an invisible foe. He closed his eyes and for a moment slept, dreaming of fingers growing larger then smaller and larger again, like bloating flesh balloons.

When he woke he noticed a pungent odor and turned his head on the pillow to see incense burning in a clay olla on the floor beside him. A single candle lit the room.

Soon Malena entered in a dark robe that hung to the floor. She knelt beside him, muttering an incantation in a language he did not know, then held up a cup to him.

"Drink."

"What is it?"

"Tea."

The liquid had a raw, burning, chemical flavor but he managed to get it down as she watched. She then took stalks of strong-smelling herbs in her hand and passed them over his body and around his head as she chanted, and he realized the words were Indian. Next she did the same with an egg, circling his head with it while intoning strange words, then broke the egg into a glass of water on the mat beside him.

Nick tried to keep his eyes open so as not to return to the fever dreams with the hands that almost exploded, but he did.

Soon though he was awake again, sensing that he had not slept long. Malena had left the room, but it was still dark outside and the candle not much shorter. The ringing in his ears had lessened, the pulsing in his head had diminished, and the fever was gone. He turned and saw that the raw egg Malena had broken into the glass had cooked solid.

His eyes were closing as she came back into the room. She lay beside him and opened the robe.

The candlelight gave a soft, yellow tint to her breasts and stomach.

She pressed herself to him, straddled him as he lay on his back, and guided him into her.

"Te quiero," she said as she moved her hips. "Te quiero." And soon he let go and felt his surge rising into her.

Now his eyes closed and he felt her lie next to him and rest her head on his shoulder. Love, she had proclaimed. But he felt no love within him, only a searing hatred for those who had killed his father, a hatred that overwhelmed any tender feelings he may have had for her.

Once during the night Nick woke from a nightmare, calling out, "No, Vicente. No! Don't do it!"

He felt Malena's lips at his ear and her warm breath.

"Don't worry," she whispered. "Solamente sueñas. You are only dreaming."

■

It was a damn stupid thing to have happened, but it had. A mere ten-foot fall down a hidden rock face. And now he saw he might die because of it.

Pulling on a fist of vines growing up the rocks and pushing against the earth with his rifle stock gripped in the other hand, Nick managed to scoot back against the cool stones. He studied the ankle more carefully and saw bone pressing against his green canvas boot and now a ring of brown blood indicating a compound fracture.

He could still hear the pop of M-60s, M-16s, and AK-47s in the distance. This wasn't supposed to happen. The area had been cleared and all they had to do was talk the nurses and doctors out of the rat holes—Nick's job. But then they started firing, and now. . .

Maybe this was the end—alone, maimed by his own careless stupidity, in hostile reaches. The end of the bloodline. A million years of procreating and dying, generation upon generation, father to son, flesh of his flesh. But here it stops, in this acrid, hopeless land, with me. Never to return home. Only child, foolish only child, he thought, and a tear escaped down his cheek.

He cried not for himself—not just for himself—but for his father, and his father's father. Maybe even for his mother, though he remembered her only vaguely. He cried for his father's hopeful journey to the New World, his believing naively that evil could be outrun. Now Nick, with some diligence, had rediscovered it—and in doing so had likely obliterated the Petrov line in some Asian wood. A sort of satirical mandala; a divine irony devised by gods enamored with black comedy. Or maybe, he thought, it's just natural selection.

The air had grown suddenly silent. If he sat still—perfectly still—it really didn't hurt too badly. But he knew that sooner or later he'd have to move. Maybe he could lash together some kind of splint, fabricate a crutch, hobble back toward camp in hopes of first encountering another G.I. instead of more V.C. That would be his only reasonable hope. But walking five klicks seemed impossible, and now he wondered whether he should even make the effort.

His thoughts returned to his father—also in jungle this time of year, mucking about with old bones. He saw his face and heard him announce his parting words as if giving his class an assignment: "You will come back. You must. I shall trust in God to protect you from harm." A hollow hope, it was now apparent. The old bastard had a superstitious streak for an educated man, believing in spirits, fate, luck, and divine intervention.

But Nick had learned that hopes, prayers, heartfelt wishes, and gods had little to do with who lived and who died. Things happened for material reasons. You didn't even get a scratch and your asshole buddy crouching next to you was cut in half not because you were blessed and he cursed by intervening divinities, but thanks to the physics of shrapnel. Some sons came home walking and others returned feet first not because of a preordained script or parental prayer, but because Son A kept his head down and Son B fucked up.

Nick sat in the shade of the rock face calculating how much daylight he had left and how fast he might expect himself to move. Wondering whether he would faint from the pain and whether it would be friend or foe who first spotted him. Again, just a matter of physics.

Well, Son B, Nick told himself, time to revert to Son A, to attempt, at least, not to let it all end here for no good reason—God willing.

Nine

"Take care of yourself." Those were Malena's parting words the next morning. At her door she laid her hand on his arm, fixed him with a meaningful gaze, and said, "Cuídate, Nicholas," with, he thought, unnecessary gravity.

Yet by the time he reached the hotel he had forgotten the cold feeling her eyes had given him. But then, as he was leaning around the reception desk to fetch his key from its hook on the wall, Andrés came up behind him, stared at the bandage on the back of his skull, and said:

"I am happy to see that you have returned, señor. I thought I might have to put the books back beneath the bar."

Nick faced him. Andrés stood shaking his head in a scolding, avuncular way. So he had already heard. The little man moved his head slowly from side to side. "Tenga cuidado, señor. Be careful."

Nick was getting the message.

He showered, dressed, and made his way to the Church of the Inquisition, where the funeral Mass had already begun. At the great wooden doors of the church he stood peering inside.

In front of the altar on a rustic table lay an open coffin from which rose Barbarita's profile. Francisco, his mother and daughter, Martín, and other apparent relatives sat in the front pews. Flowers and candles rested on the table at either end of the casket—now enshrouded in black cloth with rococo silver trim. A priest wearing a white robe over a black cassock stood in front of the coffin addressing the mourners.

Nick could barely hear his words and so stepped over the wooden rail into the church.

A chiseled stone in the wall to his right gave the date of construction as 1547. With forced Indian labor, most likely, Nick told himself. Usually on the site of Indian temples, which were leveled by the Spaniards, who then reused the stones in the building of churches. He remembered his father showing him Mexico City cathedrals built on Aztec holy ground and talking coolly of Cortez slaughtering thousands.

The dark, musty-smelling church was nearly filled, so Nick joined a line of mourners standing against the back wall. The priest called out over the intermittent cries of babies and the shuffling of feet.

"No podemos entender. . .We cannot understand the mysteries of life and of death. We cannot know why God chooses. . ."

Next to Nick an infant wrapped in a shawl on its mother's shoulder reached out, grasping for a lock of his blond hair. Nick smiled; the young Indian mother smiled back. Behind her, against the left wall of the church, he noticed a glass casket in which lay a life-size Christ in macabre detail: the blood a convincing translucent red, open wounds showing white sinew and purple muscle, His terrified eyes tight with pain.

". . .take this our fragile flesh. . ."

On the wall above the glass casket hung a large, horrific painting of Hell where sinners were being dismembered on a great, bloodied altar and fed into a fire. Nick thought of Aztec mass sacrifice and of churches built on the foundations of tribal temples.

"...now part Francisco and Barbara, who were joined here together..."

Nick backed out of the church. The Mass would soon end and the procession to the cemetery begin. He decided to join them there. His presence in the cortege, looming over the dark-skinned mourners, would look absurd—perhaps even comic. He did not belong here, either.

As he took one last look through the church door he saw the coffin being closed. Francisco looked at his wife for the last time. The Mass was over.

Nick strolled from the center of town through the old colonial quarter, then past the barrio bajo—lower both on the hill and the social scale—and down the unpaved road toward the cemetery. As he walked he remembered the last time he saw his father alive, but the memory made him uncomfortable. He had been in a hurry to leave but now could not recall why.

When he had nearly reached the gates of the cemetery he turned to look for the procession. It had not yet appeared at the top of the long hill. His throat was dry and his bandaged head throbbed from the long walk over rough streets. He turned back and looked down the road past the panteón.

There he saw a mechanic's shop, a gasoline station, and, just beyond it, a sign he had missed on the Day of the Dead in all the dust kicked up by the pilgrims: "Cervecería." Nick crossed the road and moved toward it.

Through a small window on the front of the brewery he bought a beer and drank it leaning against the wall. Around him in all directions he saw arid earth, scrub, and cactus—little to relieve the hot feeling of the day. No green trees, blue lakes, or cool grass. Just rocks and dust.

By the time he finished the beer the cortege had come halfway down the hill. Nick went back to the window for another and found some shade on the far side of the building, where he sat with his bottle on the running board of a truck.

When he had downed the second beer he returned the bottle to the window and moved back across the road to the cemetery. By now the hearse had reached the bottom of the hill, followed on foot by Francisco, the priest, and the rest of the mourners. At the cemetery gates Nick saw three of Francisco's fellow drivers waiting beside their taxis. He nodded to them and passed through the gates into the panteón.

He waited in the shade of tall poplars. The procession moved slowly. Another five minutes perhaps before they got to the gates; once inside, more words from the priest; then the sealing of the crypt. It would all take a while and Nick felt the pressure of the beer building inside him.

He looked around the cemetery. Near the concrete crypts at the lower end of the panteón stood the old gravedigger he had talked with previously, awaiting Barbarita. Nick moved to his left toward the shaded grave markers.

He found a wide tree, stepped behind it, and unzipped looking over his shoulder. Then he looked down. At his feet he saw white bones pushing up through the earth, saw his piss running over the bones and mixing with the dust. He shook his head then turned to gaze down the hill toward his father's grave.

Nick moved back to the gates as the cortege approached and could now hear the wailing of the family. But as the procession neared the gates he saw the hearse veer close to the ditch at the side of the road and the mourners squeeze together behind it. Nick heard music playing and turned.

Coming over the hill past the cervecería rolled a rusted red truck pulling a flat-bed trailer. On the trailer rode a caged tiger, two small elephants tethered to stakes driven into the wooden trailer bed, and a camel. Prancing clowns, dwarves, jugglers, and scantily-clad acrobats followed the trailer. From a loudspeaker atop the cab of the truck a booming voice enthused, "The Magic Circus has arrived at Escondido!"

As the two processions passed one another, shoulders almost touching, the music abruptly stopped, the ringmaster's voice fell silent, and the anguished cries of the mourners abated. The only noise Nick perceived was that of feet tramping through the dust.

Through their tears the mourners gaped at the animals and looked the passing performers up and down. The circus marched solemnly by—acrobats with heavy tread, jugglers' arms limp at their sides, clowns with shoulders drooping—all casting sidelong glances at the cortege and the casket inside the hearse.

Once the two processions had passed one another, the old women behind the hearse began again to wail, clowns and dwarves resumed their jaunty, skipping pace, and the jugglers hurled hoops and clubs into the air. After a moment the music again blared from the loud-speaker and soon faded in the distance as the circus moved up the hill toward the town center.

Nick stood just inside the cemetery walls. As the front end of the hearse—merely an old station wagon painted black—appeared at the gate, a sudden blast from the horns of the taxis parked on the other side of the wall made Nick start.

The horns howled on as the hearse moved past him—quickly, it now seemed. Behind came the family, heads bent forward, faces held in the crooks of left elbows, right hands reaching out as if to touch the tailgate of the hearse, Francisco in a black shirt and Martín and their mother and the others all in black, moving blindly through the gate, moaning, wailing, tears coursing down their cheeks and dropping into the dust, all to the eerie howling of taxi horns. Nick folded his arms across his chest as he felt a chill run up them and down his spine.

Then he fell in behind the cortege and followed it to the concrete crypts at the bottom of the hill.

Martín and the other pallbearers pulled the coffin from the hearse and set it on the ground. The priest spoke briefly over it. Then they lifted the coffin to the third level of a row of attached concrete crypts and pushed it into place.

The old gravedigger stepped forward, setting a weathered footstool before the crypt next to a pile of orange bricks and a plastic yellow bucket filled with mortar. The mourners watched silently and intently as he took a trowel in his right hand.

Short white stubble covered the haggard brown face of the gravedigger, who wore a soiled straw hat and tattered trousers. He scratched the stubble on his chin and bent to retrieve a brick. The old man stepped onto the stool, plopped down some mortar, and laid a brick in place. Then he stepped down to get another orange brick and repeated the process. When the opening was covered he took more mortar and slapped it over the bricks to seal the crypt. The cemetery sat silent except for the sound of wet concrete plopping into place and the scrapings of the trowel.

Then with fluid sweeping motions the gravedigger smoothed the concrete as if erasing Barbarita's life. Nick saw a look of seeming glee in the old man's eyes, as though a faithful servant of Death.

Francisco stepped forward and handed the gravedigger a scrap of paper. With his finger the old man copied into the soft mortar the dates and name of Barbara Josephina Rodriguez de Rosales. Then he stepped down.

Francisco again moved forward, this time laying a lone rose on the ledge of the crypt below her name. It was over.

As the mourners turned to march back up the hill, Nick moved toward the line of wooden crosses stuck in the earth nearby. But when he got halfway to his father's grave he stopped, put his hands in his pockets, and stood thinking, trying to remember why he had been in such a hurry when they last parted.

"Señor. . .Señor."

He turned. Francisco's mother stood before him, rosary clutched in her hands, a black shawl encircling the sharp, Indian face. Her eyes darted from side to side and her lips moved as though searching for words. She took his hand softly in hers.

"You. . .You were sent by God."

A sob broke from the woman, and Nick reached out to steady her. As Martín came up behind his mother and placed his hands on her shoulders, she turned her face into his chest. Martín nodded to Nick and led her away. Nick glanced once more over his shoulder at the wooden crosses, then began walking back up the hill toward the cemetery gates.

He saw Francisco also moving up the hill from the crypt hand-in-hand with his daughter. When they met at the gate the two men shook hands and Francisco patted his daughter's head.

"Do you remember Señor Nicholas, Angelita?"

The child nodded and her father looked up at Nick. A light breeze swayed the poplars along the cemetery wall and ruffled their leaves. Francisco said, "If there's ever any way I can help you, Nicholas, I am ready."

Nick nodded and they again shook hands. He turned and made his way alone back up the dusty road toward the center of town. Sent by God. He blew out a short breath and the dust from the road made him cough.

As the door to the office clicked, Nick started. He straightened himself on the bench where he had dozed off and rubbed his eyes. Coming out the door was a thin campesina with dark circles under her eyes. Wrapped in a rebozo at her breast an infant slept and another child—a boy perhaps three years old in ragged, unwashed trousers— clung to her long skirt.

Nick saw the silhouette of a man through the frosted glass at the top half of the polished wooden door and heard a deep voice.

"Sí, Señora Gonzalez, we are continuing our search. Do not lose hope. In the meantime I am sure there are friends who can help you."

The woman edged her way over the polished floor, staring at it with vacant eyes. The voice continued:

"Believe me, we are doing our best. This morning I telephoned the governor personally about expanding our search to other states. Your husband will be found, I promise you."

As the door opened wider Nick saw Chief of Police Hernandez with one hand on the door knob and the other ushering the woman out of his office. He smiled and tugged the ear of the child at her side. Behind that child three more filed out, a girl and two boys. The oldest son, perhaps eight, wore no shoes. The children's faces were splotched with grime and, as they passed, Nick caught the smells of earth and smoke—and a stale human odor that made him hold his breath.

Hernandez nodded toward Nick, who rose from the bench and marched past the chief into the office. Hernandez pulled the door closed behind him, shaking his head.

"Pobrecita. A month now since she has seen her husband. There is no food and no family to help them, so they must beg on the streets and scavenge at the market for rotten food."

Hernandez indicated a wooden chair across from his large mahogany desk and Nick sat.

"And the husband?"

The chief moved around the desk and sat back in his swivel chair, folding his hands across a large brass belt buckle. The black leather holster and revolver he had worn into La Última Cena hung on a hat tree in the corner. Hernandez shrugged.

"Quién sabe? Maybe he got drunk and fell into an arroyo. Perhaps he won the lottery and ran off with another woman. People come and go. It is a free country."

Hernandez wore a mustache and full head of hair almost too black for a man of fifty-five. The face was puffy but not unpleasant, the eyes those of an indulgent priest.

"Now, Mr. Petrov, how can we help you?"

"You know my name. Then you probably know that my father died here last month."

Hernandez pursed his lips and nodded. "I also know of your conversation with Dr. Sanchez early this morning. So you now believe your father died wrongfully and you wish for my office to investigate. Am I correct?"

Nick opened his mouth to speak but Hernandez went on:

"I would very much like to help you, but officially I have no reason to do so, and therefore no authority."

"But Dr. Sanchez. . ."

"Last month Dr. Sanchez signed the autopsy report swearing to its accuracy. He will continue to do so."

"Of course. Nonetheless you know what Dr. Sanchez told me. That it was Vicente's men who brought him the body and suggested the outcome of the autopsy."

"Officially I know only what I have read in the autopsy report. I cannot commit the limited resources of my office on hearsay."

Nick let out a long breath.

"Okay. But if the body were exhumed and reexamined and evidence could be found. . ."

"Then I would be happy to investigate. As it stands I am bound by the sworn statement of the doctor. And, as there is no other evidence . . ."

"Can we exhume the body to get the evidence?"

"Of course."

Nick leaned forward.

"When?"

"Whenever you can obtain an authorization from your embassy. Then you can do with the body as you please. You can have a second autopsy performed in Mexico City—or in the United States if that would satisfy you."

Nick nodded and continued nodding. "I see. Then you have no interest in the irregularities of my father's death. The fact that Vicente had. . ."

Hernandez held up his hand.

"Momentito, señor. Irregularities? First, do you know what is regular here? And second, is it possible that your father—an older man who is unaccustomed to the altitude—has a few drinks, clutches at his chest, and collapses? His drinking companions take him to the doctor but it is too late. He is dead. Naturally they say, 'He died of a heart attack. We saw it. And please, do not mention us. We do not wish to become involved with the gringos.' Is that possible?"

Hernandez leaned forward and put his folded hands on the desk top. "I also saw your father's body. There was nothing to indicate any violence."

Nick looked out the window to his right at a barren plaza. There was nothing to see but he looked anyway. Then he turned back to Hernandez.

"There are many ways to kill a man. A thorough autopsy should have been performed as my government requested. Now it will be."

As Nick stood so did Hernandez.

118

"As you wish."

But, as Nick started toward the door, Hernandez added: "One more thing. Some advice. It would please me if you could avoid the bars and cantinas during the rest of your stay here, for your own good—and mine. I also do not wish to become involved with your government."

Nick snorted and pulled open the door.

"Petrov. . ."

Nick turned in the doorway and looked back at Hernandez, who stood beside his desk slowly patting the paunch that hung over his belt buckle.

"Cuidado, señor. Be very careful."

Malena and Nick followed the distant circling lights through the still night to a dusty lot on the lower side of town where a large, khaki-colored tent had been erected. Over the entrance to it a lighted sign read, "El Circo Mágico."

From the back of the tent they watched a tightrope walker, a contortionist, and dwarves cavorting with yapping dogs. The heavy air inside the tent filled with the screams of children and their high-pitched laughter. As the lion tamer was announced Malena and Nick stepped back outside.

They walked among well-used carnival rides. An old carousel, a small Ferris wheel, mock helicopters circling slowly. The children on the rides laughed freely and Nick felt a sudden melancholy.

"This reminds me of another time," he said, "of my childhood."

"De veras? In the United States?"

"Truly."

A young couple passed arm-in-arm—the girl, perhaps fifteen, already pregnant, her man not much older. They kissed unashamedly, and Nick saw Malena lift an eyebrow as though in disapproval.

At jerry-built booths, Indian women sold sliced fruits, popcorn, and fried meats. Nearby, other vendors hawked ices, jicama, and roasted peanuts. An old man in a straw sombrero offered pastel cookies—pink, orange, chartreuse—in a basket set on a collapsible wooden stand, but no one was buying. He moved along and set up his stand ten feet away as though a subtle shift in location might change his luck.

They bought two ice creams and stopped at a booth to watch young boys attempt a seemingly impossible game of chance, trying to toss thin metal washers over nails hammered into an unpainted board.

Under a blue tent whose sides were rolled up to its top, a bingo game was under way. Women and children sat at benches on the circumference studying their cards, the prizes hanging from strings above their heads: tin pots, plastic buckets, brushes. The caller stood by a bin in the center of the tent and Nick thought he heard him call "el burro". Moving closer Nick saw that instead of numbers and letters the cards bore pictures of familiar items—a donkey, the sun, a cactus, the Devil. When an object was called, its picture was covered with a kernel of corn.

Nick felt moved by the scene—by the homely prizes and earnest looks on the players' faces—and somehow saddened. Malena, however, fidgeted impatiently, as though embarrassed by the un-sophisticated setting. Nick looked at his watch and said, "I must go."

"Where?"

"To De Efe on tonight's train. But I promise to return in a day or two."

He waited for her to ask why he was going, a question he did not want to answer right now. But instead she merely said, "I can go with you if you wish—I know the capital well. But I do not like it."

"Then stay here. I won't be away long."

"Bueno. And though you are far, our spirits will continue to talk."

When he walked her to her door and kissed her, Malena wet her finger on her tongue and pressed it to his forehead as though casting a spell to protect him on his journey. Nick moved up the hill to the zócalo wondering how well her magic actually worked.

Luis and Miguel were in the hotel bar drinking. When they saw Nick at the reception desk they raised their glasses to him from across the courtyard and smiled. Nick did not smile and did not wave back.

Andrés came scurrying from behind the bar, crossed the patio, and scooted to the other side of the reception. Nick told him, "I am leaving, Andrés. Please prepare my bill. I will go upstairs to pack and return in a moment."

Andrés glanced at the men in the bar and nodded.

"It is best."

A taxi sat waiting at the sitio in the zócalo. Nick approached with his suitcase and saw that the driver was a thin, unshaven man he did not know.

"To the train station."

When they arrived the station was again dark and no one else awaited the train. Nick handed folded notes over the seat back to the driver.

"Are you able to wait? The train may be late or perhaps never come."

The cabby raised his hands palms up. "Lo siento. I have another fare to pick up in ten minutes." He pointed to his watch as if to give evidence for his claim. "But I will return in a half hour to see if the train has arrived."

Once again Nick sat on his upended suitcase on the station platform, this time perfectly alone. He sat thinking about Malena's magic
—which she said he shared—and the Magic Circus. He thought about
the children on the merry-go-round and the faces of the bingo players,
about how simple life might be. And about how complex and distasteful was much of the world he knew. Which made him think of Luis
and Miguel sitting in the bar, and soon he was jumping at noises in the
dark.

The cabby never returned and the train was an hour and a half
late.

■

Nick signaled the waiter for another beer and turned back to his father, who sat looking at him appraisingly across the table, his eyes moving over his son's uniform jacket then rising again to his gaunt face.

"Yeah, I know," said Nick. "I'm not eating enough and drinking too much. Well, hell. We're celebrating, aren't we?"

His father nodded. "Yes, we are. It is good to have you home in one piece."

Nick pulled a crooked smile. "Thanks to a few nuts and bolts."

"Now what, Nicholas? I mean after you're discharged. What will you pursue? Have you decided?"

Nick recognized what restraint his father was exercising, waiting until after dinner to broach the subject and then not starting off by browbeating him on the joys of chasing obscure academic phantoms.

"Pursue? I'm dead tired of pursuit. I don't know. I haven't thought much about the future, just about getting this far."

The professor nodded. "Of course. I understand."

Nick gulped down more beer and pushed his half-empty plate away. His father leaned forward slightly.

"Over Christmas break I'll return to the Quintana Roo site I wrote you about. The ruins we're working are magnificent. We've found tombs entirely intact...Why not come with me? Just like old times, Nicholas."

Nick tapped a Pall Mall on his watch face, placed it in the corner of his mouth, and lit it with a Zippo.

"That's jungle, ain't it? I don't know. I've been mucking around ass-deep in swamp water for a whole year. And ruins. Out in the middle of the fucking jungle you come across these Buddhist temples or shrines or whatever from a thousand years ago. And a thousand years from now when we're long gone they'll still be standing. Like you once told me: our living or dying makes no difference except to ourselves."

Nick's eyes avoided his father's gaze, focusing on the plate where he rolled gray ash from his cigarette. After a moment his father said:

"No, Nicholas. Not true. Yes, our individual living or dying may not appreciably alter the course of civilization, but it makes a great difference to those around us. I am glad you have lived through your ordeal. You know that my prayers were with you. . ." Then, as if reminded, "Will you come to Mass with me tomorrow?"

Nick shook his head. "Mumbo jumbo. You told me not to believe in unsubstantiated theories. I've followed your advice."

"You don't have to believe, Nicholas. Just go for the ritual, for the peace, for the comfort to your soul."

Nick took a drag on his cigarette, exhaled white smoke through his nostrils, and shook his head. "Even if I had a soul, I doubt it could be comforted."

Ten

Nick stood on the platform between the clacking coaches watching the sun rise to a clear day. He had slept fitfully in the airless car and woke for good while it was still dark. Now he watched the sun climb over the arid land, where a man plowed a dusty field behind an ox.

His dreams had not been good. He couldn't quite remember them, just knew they hadn't been good. The usual probably. Once in the night he woke in a sweat with heart pounding and found the man across the aisle of the coach staring at him.

Despite the cloudless day, as the train reached the outskirts of the capital the sky began to darken. When Nick stepped outside the terminal to find a taxi and looked up, he could not see the sun, only a circular, yellow-gray glow behind a gauze of smog.

As he waited for a cab, suddenly a rooster crowed behind him, and he whirled to see the woman next in line tucking the bird's head back inside a plastic sack. The artless rooster didn't realize that he was being brought to a place where his kin, the wild birds, fell dead from the trees, asphyxiated.

Nick passed the letter and attached autopsy report across the desk to a man who lifted to his nose a pair of half-moon reading glasses not unlike those Nick's father had worn. His eyes moved back and forth across the page. He flipped the letter over energetically and studied the autopsy report. With eyes still on the document he announced, "Everything here seems to be in order. . ."

Nick waited until the man raised his eyes from the paper and gazed at him over the top of the spectacles. A thin man with graying hair and tasteful gray suit, button-down collar, striped tie. On the wall behind him hung a photo of the U.S. president.

"Exactly," said Nick. "It *seems* to be in order. But that's the intent of the falsification, to give the appearance of a natural death. As I said, the doctor himself told me. He was asked not to delve into the cause of death and simply to attest that it resulted from a heart attack. The paperwork I have no argument with. It's what that paper conceals that interests me."

"The doctor himself told you this?"

"Right."

"Why on Earth would he disavow his own sworn statement?"

Nick skewed his mouth to the side. The interview brought back a feeling he had not had since Nam, where more than once he had to fabricate a plausible explanation for a bungled field operation without revealing the truth, that cynical soldiers had improvised their own self-serving and life-preserving script to circumvent official orders that had the ring of danger and death.

"I caught him off guard. I guess he was embarrassed."

"Embarrassed? How?"

"Well, I had learned—or surmised actually—that his negligence had caused the death of my friend's wife, on whom he had operated."

"American?"

"Mexican."

"So you used that knowledge to blackmail this Dr. . .uh. . ."—he looked through this glasses at the report—". . .Sanchez and got him to say that your father's autopsy report was faulty."

"No, not faulty, falsified. No autopsy was performed."

"As the doctor has said—under duress."

Nick looked at the picture of the president and took a deep breath. The embassy man continued:

"But even if the doctor is now telling the truth you still have nothing except your intuitions to indicate there was anything unnatural about your father's death."

"Look. My father was in perfect health. No bad heart, no problems of any sort. Next thing he's dead in a backwater Mexican town and there's a cover-up under way."

The embassy man took the glasses off his nose.

"I see no evidence of any cover-up nor misfeasance of any sort in our conduct in this matter. We sent a man out for identification, we..."

"I meant the autopsy report. Only that. The embassy did its job. It's not to blame. I know you have to rely on local officials. All I need now is an exhumation order and transit papers to get the body into the States."

"You should have had the body shipped back before it was buried."

"I was in Paris on vacation. It took them two weeks to track us down. By that time he was already in the ground."

But as Nick said it he felt a twinge of guilt. It had been his last chance to return with his father to the places the old man loved most, where they had spent summers together when Nick was a child. And Nick had passed on the offer without even giving it serious consideration.

"As far as the exhumation and transit orders are concerned there shouldn't be a problem. I'll contact the Gobernación today. You have a right to the body. But as to any official involvement by the embassy in a secondary autopsy. . ."

"Right. Just cut the papers."

"Of course, if a new autopsy were to indicate something irregular in your father's death, see that we're properly notified. We'll take over from there. But as to your continuing personal involvement in such a case, that we cannot condone. That's what we're here for. We're quite well organized.

"In the meantime, I suggest you be more scrupulous about your activities while in Mexico. Remember you are not in the United States. If you run afoul of Mexican laws—and they do have laws against blackmail—you're on your own.

"Stop back first thing tomorrow and we'll have your papers for you."

He rose, walked Nick to the door, and paused as he reached for the handle.

"Mr. Petrov...I wonder if I might ask you a personal question... How close were you to your father?"

Nick felt his heart suddenly racing, as if he had been caught in a lie. He tried to sound casual instead of guilty.

"Why do you ask?"

"Maybe there was a health problem you weren't aware of. Something he was keeping from you."

Nick stared at the gray carpet trying to remember that last evening together and whether his father had tried to tell him something.

Nick paused outside the embassy security fence where a Marine stood guard, feeling that he had had enough of America for one day. Damn well organized.

He gazed down the Reforma at the tall palms that lined the street in perfect rows all the way to Chapultepec, the grass on the islands between the flow of traffic lush green. Gleaming office towers, chic apartment buildings, and expensive hotels faced the street. From his prospect it might have been a European capital.

Nick crossed the Reforma suitcase in hand into the Zona Rosa, where there was more of the same: stylish restaurants and hotels, expensive boutiques. He booked a room at the old Géneve, whose lobby was not as he remembered it from childhood, and left his bag at the desk.

He walked to the nearby Insurgentes metro station and descended. When the next train pulled in, Nick boarded, not sure where he was going. He felt a need to move, to get away from all that was straight, orderly, organized, and dead.

The subway snaked beneath the sinking city built on the soft bed of the lake surrounding Moctezuma's stronghold of Tenochtitlan. The metro tracks twisted around the visible tops of pyramids now buried beneath the capital. Above ground, he knew, twenty million people went about their daily movements, skimming over the world of their ancestors below.

Soon he detrained, following a crowd up into the gray daylight— grayness in all directions, the snow-capped mountains surrounding the city no longer visible through the smog. Nick found himself strolling about an immense market where food to help feed the twenty million came in daily.

The surrounding streets and alleyways were crowded with vendors, laborers, acrobats, snake-handlers, drunks, whores, beggars, and cripples, seeking a customer, a job, a handout, a meal. Not the fashionably dressed cosmopolitans of the Zona Rosa but the masses, the working class, a short, dark people whom Nick towered over, and it was nothing like Europe.

He heard the penetrating calls of hawkers, the squawks of caged birds, the roar of trucks, the groans of livestock being led to slaughter. He saw a rainbow of ripe fruits and vegetables, wine-colored meats, a spectrum of beans and chiles, all displayed for sale. But the odors of the market dominated. Rotting produce, fresh flowers and fish, frying flesh, cheap perfume, manure, the piss of dogs and men, and perspiration. Always perspiration.

He meandered through the roofed market watching the mestizos heaving sacks onto their backs, loading and unloading the trucks, sweeping, bending, lifting. He thought of the man behind the ox whom he had glimpsed from the speeding train and of the sweat of field hands, farmers, and fishermen, all of those whose perspiration hung on every mango and mackerel, on every loaf of bread and brick of the city. It's what seemingly kept the sinking city perilously afloat: perspiration.

After an hour of wandering through the market, its side streets, and its alleys, he had had enough. Too many strange sights, too many people pressing too close together, too many smells. But the thought of squeezing into a stuffy subway car with a throng of perspiring people now appalled him. Instead he hailed a taxi and went directly to his hotel, comfortably alone.

Opening the door to his room he saw his suitcase sitting on a stand next to the bed. He closed the door behind him and moved to a small refrigerator by the dresser. Inside he found liquors, beer, wine, Champagne. He took out a bottle of white Baja wine and opened it with a corkscrew chained to the side of the refrigerator.

He sat in a cushioned chair with his feet on the bed, perfectly alone, sipping the wine, resting in the clean quiet of the air-conditioned room, feeling now more at home.

■

"This is good news. I'm glad you decided to continue your studies. I shall talk to the registrar."

Nick let out a sigh. It seemed that breathing was always difficult in the cramped apartment.

"Thanks, but I need to get away. I've decided to go to the state university."

His father looked at him, incredulous. "I thought you wanted an education."

"It's good enough."

"No, it's not good enough. It is second rate—third rate."

"It's the only thing I can afford on the G.I. bill."

"If you had studied instead of wasting your youth you could have had a scholarship anywhere. But as it stands I am willing to help you."

"I don't need your help."

The elder Petrov raised an eyebrow. "So it seems. You have always rejected my aid—as though your father was an embarrassment to you."

At his father's words Nick sensed hot blood rushing to his face. For whatever reasons that's what he felt, that his father was an anachronism, some sort of hoary, slow-moving intellectual dinosaur in world built on action and speed.

"It's just that I'd rather do it on my own."

"That too is typical of a young man intent on differentiating himself from his father—Freud was right enough about that."

"I'm nothing like you." Nick heard his voice thicken with anger.

A heavy silence fell over the two men as Professor Petrov filled his pipe. Nick lit another cigarette and tossed the red pack on the dining room table where they sat. Then he reached for the bourbon and poured himself another shot.

Finally his father put a match to the pipe and, as puffs of sweet-smelling smoke encircled him, said, "So you want to be on your own. Perhaps that would be best. Maybe what we need here is distance. You know, you could study abroad and in that way be free of my importuning."

"I've been abroad."

"Yes, but Saigon is hardly Heidelberg. A few years at a top European university would catapult you ahead of your American peers."

"Yeah, the ones hiding in libraries."

"So now you tell me that you not only plan to go to the public university but also to eschew books?"

Nick saw that it was no good talking about it. He always fell into his father's logical traps, and his father could never understand the inexpressible urge Nick had for. . .for what? Perhaps to experience life firsthand instead of through the filter of his father. To do something that would use up his anger. Nick had trouble putting a finger on it. But he knew he would not find what he wanted in dusty stacks at the library.

"I don't want to live in the past. I'm fed up with dead thoughts and dead men. I've had enough of it."

"Then what will you study—the non-existent future?"

"I was thinking about journalism."

His father's eyebrows shot up. He sucked on his pipe and shrugged.

"Why go to university at all? Return instead to grammar school so you can write like a child. Then you can venture forth documenting all the tedious minutiae of life."

"Instead of documenting the minutiae of death?"

His father went on as if deaf to Nick's parry:

"A good waste of your talents, that. Why must everything be new and immediate? You are being seduced by another illusion, Nicholas."

Nick sat silent, grinding teeth, not knowing how to defend himself against the one man who knew all his vulnerabilities. His father shook his head and continued:

"There is nothing new, Nicholas. We are essentially the same as we were a hundred or a hundred thousand years ago, just using different tools. We retain the same basic wants, the same urges, the same primal satisfactions. . .You think I delude myself by studying dead men and ancient artifacts but you are wrong, Son. It is all there—all the secrets, all the answers you seek—for what is valuable endures. But I suppose that every man must learn it for himself."

Nick took another pull on his whiskey glass before responding.

"That's not what I see enduring in our progressive century. No, what I see is Verdun, Dachau, Hiroshima, My Lai. Your intellectual certainty doesn't matter a damn these days. Power matters. Strength matters. That's all that endures because it's the victor who defines what's valuable. You're the only one who cares about the past. The rest of us are trying to forget it."

Alexander Petrov sat at the far end of the table studying his son. But Nick, as usual, could perceive little sign of emotion behind the stoic mask of his father.

Then his father said, "I see how you might think that, Nicholas, given your experience. But these times are not so different from those that came before. If you would deign to listen to the dead they would tell you all you need to know in order to live."

Nick sniffed and sucked at his whiskey. Dead men talking. That was rich. The old man's losing it, he thought. Been digging around in old bones just too damn long.

Eleven

The train never came to a complete stop. When it slowed into Escondido at the hottest time of day, Nick jumped onto the platform, and the diesel resumed speed, blowing black smoke.

As he looked around him he saw that no one else had detrained and no taxi waited. Squinting up at the afternoon sun he placed his suitcase atop his head and began the trek to town.

At the zócalo he bought a plastic cup of guayaba juice under the portales and drank it sitting on a shaded bench. A man passed handing out leaflets. Nick grabbed the one held out to him and read,

Sábado

3 Toros

Listed below were the names of the toreros and the location of the bullfight, a small ring at the edge of town. But Nick scoured the handbill unsuccessfully for the time of the first corrida.

He spied the man with the leaflets not far away, chatting with a group of men on the corner, and waved the announcement at him.

"Oye! At what time does it begin?"

The man studied a leaflet, looked up to Nick, and shrugged.

"When the bulls are ready to die," he said, and the others laughed.

Nick stuffed the bill into the back pocket of his jeans and crossed the zócalo to the hotel. Inside he left his suitcase with Andrés at the reception.

"So you have returned. Will you be staying long?"

Nick looked at him. He was unaccustomed to life in a small town, where everyone knew your comings and goings.

Nick retreated back through the front door to the street, wound his way through the narrow calles under the hot sun, and soon was knocking at Malena's casita.

She came barefoot to the door carrying a garden trowel in her hand and wearing a wrap-around skirt with white sleeveless blouse. Her hair was tied back with a red scarf, her face damp and flushed. When she saw it was he, she stood on tiptoes and placed a prim kiss on his chin.

Nick pressed his lips to her cheek. She smelled of earth and tasted of salt and the warmth of her body against his made his breath quicken. He lifted her in his arms and carried her inside, kicking the door closed behind him.

"Ay! What will the neighbors think," she protested meekly.

She felt surprisingly light and fragile as he carried her across the room toward the chimenea. There he placed her upon the cushions and palm-frond mat that covered the floor, slid her skirt up to her waist, and saw that she was naked underneath. When he put his hands between her thighs he found them hot and moist.

She stared into his eyes, moving her head slowly from side to side. "Last night you came to me in my dreams and carried me thus, placing me on an altar, and. . ."

Her eyes rolled back into her head and she fell limp beneath him, as though in a trance.

Malena lay on her back with her head on his chest; his arm draped across her just below her breasts. With his wrist he could feel her heart beating. Then he heard a sound, a sound like the sea.

135

"What was that?"

"What?"

"Escucha. Listen."

They lay motionless and it came again. He distinguished a crowd's roar, then whistles and catcalls. Nick turned his head and saw his pants lying within reach. From the back pocket he fished the folded handbill and passed it to her.

She unfolded it and, as she read, asked: "Do you enjoy the bull-fights?"

"I have seen them only once, in Mexico City, and that was many years ago. I'm not sure I'd like it now."

"We can go if you wish."

"Why not? If I don't like them killing the animals, I can cheer for the bull."

Malena was pulling her blouse over her head and searching for her skirt.

"Yes, you can do that. But be prepared for a disappointment."

They bought tickets for the shade at a window outside the arena and two cups of beer under the grandstand. As they climbed to their seats Nick focused on the narrow concrete steps. Then he heard a voice rasping English and looked up to see Vicente, eyes hidden behind dark glasses, sitting—alone for once—in the concrete stands, elbows resting on knees, a cup of beer in his hands.

"When I learned you left town," he said, "I hoped you would not return."

Nick stopped next to him. "Yes, I went to the capital but the air was unhealthy."

Vicente smiled. "But there at least you were breathing."

Malena held tight to Nick's arm, trying to lead him on up the stairs. He pulled it free and leaned down toward Vicente, cocking his head.

"I'm sorry, I couldn't hear you. Is something wrong with your throat?"

Vicente stood, tearing off the sun glasses. Nick saw his eyes taking him in, saw the fat man's face color. Though inches shorter than Nick, Vicente was a thick man, but soft. Nick smiled.

"Okay, *Don* Vicente," he said. "Let's see how macho you are without your two putos."

Vicente's nostrils quivered. Nick stood loose and balanced on the balls of his feet but saw that Vicente was not ready. Finally, the Mexican put his sun glasses back on, smiled, and shook his head.

"You refuse to learn our customs, how things are done in México." He lifted his chin toward the bull ring. "Watch the corrida. It may help you understand."

Vicente sat and turned back to the ritual in the center of the arena. Nick and Malena moved on to find their seats. As they climbed she said, "Suddenly I feel very cold. Something bad awaits us."

As the corrida unfolded, the memory of his previous bullfight came back to him. He recalled sitting in the sun with his father and relishing the taunting and killing of the bulls—as most boys instinctively enjoy hunting, fishing, and field trips to the slaughterhouse. But now. . .Now it was different.

And it wasn't just because these were younger, less skilled matadors and thinner, less ferocious bulls than before. Nor was it that the small town event lacked the pageantry and grandeur of the Plaza México. It was not that at all. But it had changed for him.

Now Nick winced at the piercing of the bull's shoulder by the picador, felt his stomach twist sickly at the thrust of the banderillas, and at the kill—when the mincing matador rammed the long, curved sword over the animal's now safely drooping head and horns, and Nick heard a hollow groan, a death call, echoing out from somewhere deep inside the animal and saw a spasmodic gushing of blood from the bull's nose and mouth before its legs finally buckled and it lay down carefully, like an old woman going to bed—at the kill, he felt only disgust.

Shortly the next corrida began. The bull came charging out chasing the flashing capes of the toreros. The mounted picador and the banderilleros drew blood; the matador appeared in the ring. And Nick found himself praying that the bull would ram its horns into the guts of the strutting little man in the tight pink pants and spill them onto the dust. But Malena was right. He could cheer for the bull if he wished, but this was not to be the bull's day. They did not play by the bull's rules. He had been suckered into the arena only to be slaughtered, and Nick felt suddenly empty and exposed.

"Vámonos, Malena. I have seen enough."

They left the arena and the cheering crowd behind, walking each with an arm wrapped around the other back down the street to Malena's house, neither speaking, both listening to the noise of the crowd grow fainter:

"Olé!. . .Olé!. . .Olé!. . .Olé!. . ."

Nick undressed and ran hot water in the shower. He stepped in and let it run over his head, then turned to let it beat against the back of his neck and felt the muscles there relaxing.

He heard the door to the bath open and shut, and Malena drew back the shower curtain to step in naked beside him. She turned him around, soaped his back, and rubbed it with a coarse sponge.

He told her, "You have changed much. Muchísimo. Earlier you were shy."

"It is because of you. Your magic has changed me. The señorita you took to your room no longer exits."

Nick recalled what the white-bearded gringo had said. Everyone's elusive here; everything is something else eventually.

She turned him around to face her and began soaping his chest, pushing aside the jade Kukulcan. After a minute he took the soap from her and glided it over her neck and breasts. She closed her eyes, standing with arms hanging loosely at her sides. Her near-black hair glistened with water, white droplets standing on her brown shoulders. Nick saw that she was a beautiful woman, though, as she said, perhaps not the same woman he had first met.

"Nicholas. . ." she said and paused. "Perhaps it would be better to return the jade to Vicente. Then he would leave us alone. I will get you another that is ours only."

"Did he speak to you about it again when I was in the capital?"

She hesitated then said, "No. Since the other night, no."

Nick figured that was not the case but also figured it didn't much matter. It seemed most everyone in Mexico lied. To spare feelings, to save face, to keep from saying 'No'. Now he would do the same. There was no point in giving the jade back. He'd soon be gone. On Monday morning he'd present the exhumation papers to Hernandez. Then, as quickly as possible, take the body with him on the train—perhaps even the next day. But he didn't want to talk about leaving. It served no good purpose. Besides, in Mexico intentions were at least as ephemeral as life itself.

He answered, "Do you believe that the bad blood between Vicente and me would go away if I returned the Kukulcan?"

She shrugged.

He went on: "No, bonita. It would do no good. It would only make me appear weak. You know there is more than the jade between Vicente and me. I know of nothing that can make the bad blood go away."

"Your anger will eat your soul, Nicholas. You believe Vicente has wronged you but you do not know for sure. It only makes trouble for us. I do not want bad things to come between us."

He did not want to think that in a few days' time he would leave her, that his gringo insistence on truth would be the thing that came between them.

They dried each other with a dark towel and he followed her to the bedroom, watching the way the muscles in her legs and buttocks moved. No, he did not want to think about leaving.

She had prepared a picnic for them on her palm-frond bed: hard rolls, Chihuahua cheese, thin slices of dark ham, mango. The wine was a blend of carignane and cabernet grapes from Querétaro. They sat naked on the mat, and Nick pulled the cork from the bottle and poured two glasses. Malena raised hers and said, "A nosotros."

"To us."

The wine was light and fresh tasting and good with the Serrano ham. Malena ate with her eyes on Nick, seemingly relaxed and comfortable with her own nakedness, enjoying the food and the sensual ambiance of the moment.

He said, "This reminds me of a Roman orgy."

"Yes, but better, for there is only us."

"Yes, of course, much better," Nick quickly agreed.

She studied his face for a moment then said, "I am also reminded of something else." Malena looked down into the glass of wine she held with both hands. "Do you know why I first came to you, Nicholas? Why I gave myself to you when I had given myself to no man?"

He had some guesses but shook his head.

"It's not what you think," she said, as though reading his mind. "True, there are few caballeros in Escondido, and those who do exist fear me because they believe me a witch—or because they feared my father. But no, I gave myself to you because you remind me of him."

Nick emptied his glass. That wasn't one of his guesses. He poured more wine for himself.

"He was not a rubio like you, but dark. Yet there was something in his eyes that is also in yours."

She looked up at him as though to confirm it.

"He was an old man when I was born and died before I became a woman. A big man, with shoulders like yours. He liked to sing and taught me all the songs from the Revolution and all the Mexican dances.

"My mother was twenty years younger than he—una burguesa, a bourgeois from the capital. I never understood how they came to marry. Perhaps because he was handsome in his uniform and she was young.

"But she did not like living in the provinces. When he died she took us back to the capital, where they had met. There she wore black and permitted no music, nor dancing, nor laughter in the house because of her mourning. For eight years she wore black, for eight years there was no music. That was her revenge against him for being so Mexican."

As Malena drank from her wine glass Nick moved his head slowly from side to side. But then he frowned and studied her for a moment.

"Am I your revenge on your mother? A man like your father. An outsider whom she would never choose for you."

Malena pushed aside the plates, reached across to him, and took his face in her hands.

"Do not think thus. Our meeting was fated. . .When you were gone I saw the other life in my dreams. We were in the jungle atop a pyramid; you were the holy man and I a virgin. Now our bodies have come together again across time. We shall be together until death and beyond."

Nick gazed into her dark, moist eyes and saw that she believed it to be true: together until death. It seemed impossible—implausible at best. At that moment death seemed such a long way off.

Nick looked around the lobby of the hotel for Andrés. He was not at the reception nor at the bar. Nick called aloud, "Oye! Andrés!"

But there came no reply and seemingly there was no one else around. He dug his suitcase out from behind the reception desk and crossed the zócalo with the bag on his shoulder.

In a cloudless black sky Nick saw the moon sitting atop the spire of the Church of the Inquisition. It had already been dark when he got up to leave Malena.

"Where are you going?" she had asked.

"To the hotel."

"Porqué?"

"I'm tired. I need sleep."

"It would please me if you would sleep here with me."

He continued to dress. "Bien. It would please me as well. I'll go to the hotel for my bag and return."

Now he was returning, thinking of her, of their first night together. And of their inevitable parting, which made his breath catch in his chest. Then he noticed the footsteps behind him.

Nearly to the corner where he turned onto the street that took him down the long hill to Malena's house, he looked over his shoulder into the darkness. But he could see no one.

He walked a bit faster and the footsteps behind him quickened. Nick tucked the leather suitcase under his arm and began to jog along the sidewalk.

As he turned onto Malena's street, his left foot slipped on the old, polished stones of the banqueta, twisting his ankle—the bad one—and he nearly fell. Then he squared himself and continued on, still pursued by the sound of footsteps.

As he passed under a street lamp he looked back to see who would pass beneath it next. It was then, as he was loping downhill looking over his shoulder, that something hit him across the shins.

He dove forward headlong, losing his grasp on the suitcase and hitting the sidewalk hard on his knees, chest, and chin, where he felt the skin tear away. Then they were on him.

He tried to pull himself up but his head spun and his legs were kicked from under him. A fist struck hard at his left eye and another in the small of his back—or maybe he had been kicked. He called out and a light went on nearby. The two men over him worked faster.

Nick could do nothing now but curl up, wrap his arms around his head, and hope that the light going on might cut it short. He heard a call echoing off the stucco walls and the cobblestones but could not make out what was being said. The kicking and pounding suddenly ceased.

He thought they were finished. But in the glare of the lone electric light he saw a knife blade flash, saw it dive toward him, and felt a sharp pain at his throat. He gagged and reached up as their footsteps retreated on the hard stones, knowing that his throat had been slashed.

But it hadn't. It was just that the amulet was gone.

■

It all came back to him as if but yesterday. . .The aroma of cilantro in the air, the heat of the Sunday sun, the cool concrete of the Plaza México. The crowd drunken, raucous—no work tomorrow, San Lunes, Saint Monday. A fist fight below, the combatants chided and doused with beer by those above them in the stands. His father's warm hand enveloping his own, the circle of earth at the arena floor red clay, as though tinged with blood. Then the demented, raven bull kicking at the dust; the hissed picador astride an armored horse; and the matador carrying death in his hand. The once fierce creature vanquished, the seemingly indomitable force, emblem of manic nature, now but a lifeless carcass, meat, carrion, and Nicholas felt a hot stirring in his loins and in his bowels. The same feeling that returned years later when, in an enemy tunnel seeking to coax a locale, a village name, a clue, from a Viet Cong nurse—she defiant with set jaw—his own lieutenant slid up behind her with field knife drawn and slit open her throat, her black blood spreading across the earth like that of the bull. . .But it wasn't until the following day that Nick reacted, when for no good reason one of his comrades popped a water buffalo pulling a plow through a paddy. The farmer ran as Nick slogged ankle deep to the dead animal, embracing it and sobbing after having never shed a tear for the death of any man, friend or foe, not even for his best buddy who died in his arms, nor for men he himself had killed. . .It all came back to him now as though it were yesterday. The innocence of animals, which men never possess, the innocence we mourn: childhood, Arcadia, animal nature. But why then kill the bull or buffalo, he thought, except to deny the lure of innocence—or to assert our delusion of dominion over death, unaccepting that we too are just so much flesh, awaiting the hand of our butcher?

144

Twelve

Nick lay with his head tilted back hanging over the armrest of the bench. He thought of his drinking buddies, Jaime and Raúl, and of mineral water injected into the sinuses. He thought too of the men kicking and pummeling him in the dark street and of the bull who could not comprehend the rules of the arena and stood exposed at its center.

Dr. Sanchez again bent over Nick with needle and thread in hand.

"Back a little more. . ."

Nick lifted his chin another half inch and shut his eyes tight as Sanchez breathed more whiskey into his face.

". . .Good."

The physician laced another stitch into his chin and Nick tried to hold back the tears he felt forming at the sides of his eyes. Sanchez chatted as he sewed:

"For a doctor practicing in a pueblito, medicine is more art than science. We have none of the new devices to see inside the brain or the stomach or the spine—not even an x-ray. Supplies are difficult to obtain, shipments irregular, shortages common—as with the anesthetic."

Bullshit, thought Nick, and he clamped his teeth together even harder. He talked through them.

"Not important. Chin's still numb. Can't feel a thing."

It hurt like a sonofabitch and a tear escaped from the corner of his eye and ran down his cheek. He was certain he saw Sanchez smile to himself.

Chief of Police Hernandez came walking down the hall, stopped, and tugged at his gun belt. He bent to look at Nick and what Sanchez was doing to him, shaking his head as though examining a car with a dead battery.

"When you are in one piece, come into my office."

He moved on into his office leaving the glass door ajar.

Sanchez snipped the thread.

"Sit up."

Nick pulled himself upright by grasping the back of the bench with his right hand, keeping his left elbow pressed against his side, and swinging his legs down to the floor as counterbalance.

Using a razor blade Sanchez shaved away dead skin around the left eye and put salve on the abrasion.

"You look like hell."

"Feel like hell."

"The ribs may be cracked. Have you coughed up any blood?"

"A little."

"When it gets to be more than a tablespoon let me know."

"If I am still alive."

"You are fortunate to be alive now."

Nick leaned back and shrugged.

"Just a few scrapes."

"That's not what I meant." Sanchez looked at the open door of the police chief's office and lowered his voice. "You don't know what's going on here. You may think you do, but if you ever learned. . ."

"Is that what happened to my father?"

Sanchez sucked his teeth and shook his head impatiently.

"Don't be so stubborn and stupid, gringo. This has nothing to do with you or your father. Did you get the exhumation order?"

Nick nodded.

"Then take your father's body and leave. Pronto."

Nick stared steadily at the perspiring doctor, who would of course be personally heartened by his departure and the absence of Nick's threat to expose to Francisco the doctor's culpability in Barbarita's death. "I will consider your advice."

Sanchez snapped closed his satchel and raised his voice. "There is no charge."

Nick abandoned a smile when it started to pull at the stitches in his chin. He spoke with teeth clamped shut.

"Gracias."

"See me if there are problems."

Nick tried lifting his left arm to test his rib cage and winced.

"I have no problems," he said, but Sanchez was already halfway down the hall.

Nick used the armrest to get to his feet and limped into Hernandez's office massaging his kidney. He sat across from the policeman without invitation and noticed his suitcase on Hernandez's desk. The chief leaned back in the swivel chair, his black boots beside the suitcase, hands folded behind his head. Nick spoke first.

"You know who did it, don't you?"

"I have suspicions."

"But there is nothing you can do about it, right?"

Hernandez moved his head from side to side. "Nada. Not without witnesses."

"What about the people who brought me here? Or other neighbors? Someone must have seen them?"

"No one saw a thing. No one will talk. What can I do? Before I can arrest someone, I need evidence."

Evidence. Nick looked at Hernandez without expression, thinking of the first time he saw him, when he arrested the cowboy at La Última Cena without seeming evidence.

"For example, the amulet that was stolen from me."

"Yes. That would be good evidence. If I could find the amulet it could lead me to the criminals. I have its description. I will search for it. In the meantime. . ." Hernandez nodded toward the suitcase on the desk. "The train going north comes in the afternoon. It would be best for you to be on it tomorrow."

"I haven't finished what I came for."

"Have you obtained the exhumation order? And the transport papers for the corpse?"

"In the suitcase."

"Bueno. I will personally see that the body is on the train within a week. You have my word. So there is no further reason for you to stay—and one very good reason to go: Soon I will no longer be able to protect you."

Nick looked at the chief through his swollen left eye and took in a deep breath that made his hand reach reflexively for his rib cage.

"Muchas gracias for the excellent protection you have thus far provided."

Hernandez's mustache twitched to the right and he stared at Nick for a moment. Then he swung his feet to the floor and held out his hand. "The papers."

Nick rose gritting his teeth and unlocked the small leather bag. He retrieved an envelope and handed it to the chief, who tugged out the papers folded inside and studied them.

"Believe me, Señor Petrov, there is nothing further for you to learn here about your father's death and no reason why you should not leave tomorrow.

"I know you have made friends here. Take the girl with you if you wish—she is alone. But be on the train tomorrow with or without her. For you have also made some powerful enemies."

Hernandez lowered the papers and raised his eyes. His gaze lay heavy on Nick.

"If they wished they could kill you and there would be nothing I could do. Nothing. I would be powerless to prevent it or to punish it."

Hernandez opened the center drawer of the desk, threw the papers inside, and began searching through the drawer. He spoke without looking up.

"Don't worry about tonight. As long as you leave on the train tomorrow you will not be further harmed."

Nick locked his suitcase and stared at it with a frown. Then he raised his eyes and rested them questioningly on the policeman. Finally, Hernandez pulled a long cigar from the drawer and looked up.

"Oh. Do not misunderstand me. I have no control over such things, only good information...Then we will see you at the train tomorrow? Bueno."

Nick took the suitcase by the handle and made his way slowly down the hall, out the front door of the presidencia, and onto the dark, empty zócalo.

He walked stiffly beside the white-trunked trees certain now that once he left Escondido that would be the end of it. His father's body would never be found or lost in transit or something. Nothing would ever be resolved—or, he admitted, expiated.

He was learning how things were done here. Learning of hollow promises, of people nodding sympathetically and doing nothing. He saw that they would prick him, deflect his aggression, and wear him down until he hung his head and quit—or died trying.

He moved to the taxi stand on the high side of the square, where a lone green-and-white cab sat. Nick reached through the open window of the taxi and gently shook the driver.

"Francisco, Francisco. Wake up, Pancho."

The cabby finally opened his eyes and they suddenly widened.

"Ay, chingado! What happened to your face, amigo?"

Nick turned the side-view mirror up, gazed into it, and saw that he looked much worse than he felt. He again laid his hand on Francisco's shoulder.

"Remember, Pancho, when you said that if ever you were able to help me. . .?"

She had apparently heard the cab drive up or had been watching for him and was at the door before Nick could hobble there from the taxi. In the light falling to the cobblestone street from the open doorway she saw his face and reached out to him.

"Mi amor, what have they done to you?"

Her hand found the bad ribs. He started, his breath caught in his chest, and she pulled away, bringing her hands to her face.

"No, está bien," Nick said. "Come."

He put his arm around her shoulder, leaned on her just a bit, and let her help him inside. Francisco followed with the suitcase.

She pulled chairs out from the table.

"Malena, this is Francisco. I have told you about him."

"Mucho gusto. I know your face. I am sorry for your loss. Please, sit down."

As the two men sat at the small table Malena brought a brandy bottle and two glasses from the kitchen. Nick poured for Francisco and himself as Malena stood beside him shaking her head.

"This afternoon I had the bad feeling and now I see what it was."

Nick took a swallow of brandy. "The Kukulcan is gone. They wanted that, and to punish me."

"No importa. I will find another that. . ."

Nick set his glass down on the table harder than he probably meant to.

"No, Malena. It is important. To me it is."

She shook her head slowly. "Let it go, Nicholas. You can change nothing if the gods do not will it. Your efforts will produce only evil."

Nick glanced at Francisco, who gazed back sipping his brandy without expression as though in concurrence with Malena, and Nick wondered if they weren't right. Mexico was governed by different gods—deformed gods in his view—who, unlike his omnipotent northern Creator, rewarded acceptance instead of industry, passivity instead of aggression. But those weren't his gods. Nick could not just let it go. If his efforts produced evil so be it.

"I have been ordered to leave."

"What?"

"Hernandez. He says he can no longer protect me. I have to go tomorrow on the train to the border."

She looked at him and shook her head as though in disbelief then turned to Francisco, who nodded to confirm what Nick had said. Finally, she said, "Sí. It is better to go. Hernandez knows. There is no longer a life here for us. We shall go."

He took a deep breath, his side throbbed, and he exhaled.

"No, Malena. You cannot come now. This is not yet finished."

She reached up and laid her hand over her heart.

"I will pray then that this evil will not destroy you. And that when it is finished we will be together. Forever."

Her words chilled Nick. He felt a premonition that scared him, a dark vision that lay on his shoulders like a cloud of black smoke, like a foreshadow of Death. And he found himself surreptitiously tapping the wooden table top with his knuckles as though to ward off the evil she foretold.

He nodded once to Malena then turned to Francisco.

"Mañana, Pancho, will you come to take me to the train? Good."

Francisco rose and Nick could see the question in his eyes. He would answer it tomorrow when she was not there and explain why he didn't tell her all they talked of in the taxi. But he suspected that the witch already knew.

"Hasta la mañana."

"Hasta la mañana."

Malena walked Francisco to the door. When the door closed behind him she leaned against it and gazed at Nick.

"You will go, Nicholas," she announced, "but you will return."

∎

A hell of a day to take a stroll in a cemetery, Nick had thought. Steady rain, distant thunder, and now suddenly a crack of lightning close enough to make him start, hunch his shoulders beneath his umbrella, and see artillery shells exploding.

His father, in mackintosh, brown fedora, sans umbrella, walked beside him. He must have seen Nick jump for he turned and said, "If the lightning bothers you we can go back."

Nick shook his head. "Nah. It's just the damn ankle. Damp weather's a bitch. I'm okay. . .You still come regularly or just on Easter?"

His father did not appear to have heard Nick's question.

The grass around her grave was lush green, dark and full. Nick wondered if his father took care to approach on different vectors so as not wear a path.

Standing at the foot of the grave his father closed his eyes, folded his hands, and bowed his head as if in prayer. Nick beside him dropped his eyes to the tombstone, again shaking his head. His father had still been in his thirties when Nick's mother died but bought a double plot in order to lie beside her forever—even had his name etched on the stone, wanting only his final date.

Nick couldn't figure it. The old man was a scholar, a scientist of sorts, who sought physical evidence for his theories. But he said prayers to purportedly resurrected spirits, honored gods of all ilks, and made near-weekly pilgrimages to pray over the bones of a woman two decades dead. For Nick that superstitious behavior on his father's part undermined his credibility on a score of other issues.

When Nick looked up, his father's eyes had opened and gone glassy. Professor Petrov stooped, placed upon the grave the lilies he'd bought on the way, and moved off in the direction they had come. Nick hobbled along beside him feeling the wetness of the grass saturating his shoes, sensing the dampness seeping up into the ankle held together with steel screws.

"It wouldn't hurt you to say a prayer for your mother's soul now and then."

Nick started to give his view on spiritual existence, then checked himself. What was the use of arguing? He was going his own way now. Instead he nodded and lied:

"I do at times. But you know I barely remember her. I guess that sounds bad, her only child not having warm memories. But it was so long ago and I was so young, it seems like a dream."

Yet another lie—at least in spirit. A dream, yes. But a miraculous, idyllic dream of a utopia where all was complaisant and fresh, a place of sweet perfume and fine fabrics, where the feel of warm, womanly flesh enveloped him, seeding his soul with solemnity and hope. A dream of a perpetual spring that had broken unnaturally into a stern, endless winter. His father's voice brought him back to the present:

"For me it is no dream—it is the only reality. But you have returned safely and Maria will rest more easily for it. A family once again."

Family! Nick almost laughed aloud. What good was that to him now? What he wanted was somewhere warm and dry where the metal in his leg wouldn't rust up, where ripe fruits fell sweet from laden trees, where he could lie content between a woman's breasts. No, to hell with family.

Thirteen

Francisco was leaning against the fender of the cab, looking the other way, squinting into bright sun. Malena stood in the doorway staring up at Nick, arms folded across her chest. He asked:

"Are you sure you don't want to come to the station?"

"What's the point? There is no need to say goodbye since we will be together again soon."

"Yes. Then, until that moment."

When he turned to move to the taxi she caught him by the sleeve and pulled him back toward her. As she pressed her body against his he felt her fingernails cut into his shoulder blades. Then her breath sounded in his ear with the words, "I will wait for you until death."

Only then did she release him.

Nick motioned to Francisco and jumped into the front seat of the cab with his suitcase. As Francisco started the engine Nick rolled his eyes at him. They were off.

Nick turned to wave goodbye but Malena had already gone inside and shut the door.

Nick said, "Did it go well?"

"Bien. As we discussed."

"Do we have much time?"

Francisco looked at the wrist watch hanging from the rearview mirror.

"Suficiente."

"Then let's stop somewhere for a beer. None of this is easy."

At the crossroads near the edge of town where the road to the train station met the highway, Francisco pulled the cab to the shoulder. Under two large palms sat a white wooden stand where fruits, juices, and sandwiches were sold. The shutters, hinged at the top on three sides of the small structure, were propped open with broom handles. Inside the booth stood a dark, exotic, and buxom woman, fly swatter in hand. She looked Nick up and down. He said, "Dos cervezas, por favor."

She opened two beers and set them on the counter.

They drank standing up, their backs against the counter. Behind them Nick heard the woman slapping flies. The sweet scent of her perspiration mingled with the aromas of ripe fruit and the earthy smell of the beer. Finally Nick spoke:

"It's difficult parting with a woman, even for a short time. Saying goodbye is worse than the actual separation."

Nick said the words without thinking, then realized he'd blurted them out without a thought for Francisco's endless separation from Barbarita. But the man seemed unmoved.

"You are right. It is a penalty she makes you pay for leaving her."

Nick watched a cattle truck go by spreading black smoke.

"I decided it was better to tell her nothing. I doubt that she would have approved. Certainly she would have worried. Telling her would have made it more difficult for me."

"Of course."

Nick had other reasons for not telling her but didn't want to talk about them. He wasn't sure he could have put them into words, particularly Spanish words. But he knew it would have been wrong to say anything to her about it when he himself wasn't sure what he was doing—nor why he was doing it.

When they arrived at the train station a police car was sitting beside the tracks. Chief of Police Hernandez stood on the platform in the shade of the station's eaves fanning himself with his cap and talking with a young cop twirling a nightstick.

Nick said to Francisco, "They will see me on the train one way or another."

Hernandez motioned them onto the platform as the young cop moved away. They slid out of the cab and Nick carried his suitcase up the steps.

Francisco went up to Hernandez and they shook hands. The chief patted him on the back then looked at Nick's face and frowned.

"Como estás? Is there much pain?"

"The greatest pain came at the hands of Dr. Sanchez. Now it is better."

"Everything will be better this way, Petrov. For everyone. If the train is on schedule, I will be home in time for my Sunday comida and siesta. Everything back to normal. That's how I like it."

"I have not been here long enough to see what is normal, but I do not think my stay has been typical."

Hernandez's face became suddenly solemn. His eyes flicked at Francisco for an instant.

"No, none of this is typical. I am sorry that you must leave now but you have not been wise. There is no other choice."

"I know."

"I will tend to your business here for you."

Nick glanced to his left as the sound of a diesel locomotive came vibrating up the valley. Then came another noise. The three men turned in unison and looked up the road.

A blue truck with wooden side rails came down the hill carrying on its bed a pine crate. The truck slowed, turned in a semicircle, and backed up to the tracks near the platform. Nick recognized the crate—the one containing "ancient" pottery that he had seen in Vicente's shop.

Vicente's two men climbed down from the cab and stared through sunglasses at the men above them on the platform. The men on the platform stared back.

The train appeared from behind a low hill and screeched to a stop at the platform with the sound of metal grinding on metal. The engines were kept running and the whole station shook. The doors of the baggage car slid open and the crate was loaded on. Nick took up his suitcase, shook Francisco's hand, and stepped into the old Pullman.

The train inched away. Through the open window in the door of the coach Nick saw Francisco return to his cab and drive off. Hernandez and the young cop with the nightstick got into the police car and also drove away. Luis and Miguel waited beside the truck hands on hips, watching, until the train went around a bend and Nick could no longer see whether they were still there.

The diesel regained speed slowly, seeming to strain in the afternoon heat. The first class coach sat nearly empty but Nick preferred to stand by the open window at the end of the car.

As the train reached the top of the rise and left the valley its speed began to build. Soon the railroad ties and the nopals and the magueys near the track were floating by in a blur, and the hard breeze coming through the open window made him forget the heat. He leaned against the door and looked at his watch.

Almost an hour passed before he again felt the train lurch and heard the metallic sound of the brakes. He stepped aside for the conductor to unbolt the metal door.

At a station even more dilapidated than the one at Escondido the wheels again squealed and ground to a stop. No sign to indicate the name of the pueblito, which seemed to consist of a single unpaved street and a few low, white buildings. But Nick recognized the battered white pickup truck parked just beyond the end of the platform and stepped from the train with his suitcase.

He found Martín sitting on a bench in the shade at the back of the station sipping orange soda through a straw from a plastic bag.

At sunset as they sat with beers on the fence of Martín's corral watching the sky turn pink then red, they heard a car approaching and turned to see a green-and-white taxi followed by a dust cloud crunching up the unpaved drive.

"Está Pancho. At last," said Martín.

They watched as the driver for the night shift deposited Francisco and left with the taxi. When Martín told his brother to help himself to a beer from the cooler Francisco shook his head without a word and disappeared into the house.

He maintained his silence throughout the supper of beans, sausage, and tortillas that his brother had prepared. Martín and Nick let him be. They talked about the state of the Mexican economy ("bien chingado" according to Martín), the border (also "well fucked"), and the United States ("bien loco y bien chingado tambien"). Martín then went on at length on the breeding and care of horses. But Francisco said nothing.

When the plates and empty beer bottles had been pushed aside Martín brought a dusty jug from the mantel and set it on the table along with three narrow shot glasses. He poured and said, "Salud!"

Nick sipped. "Martín, this is the best tequila I have tasted."

"I do not drink from this jug every day. But sometimes at night when the wind blows and I am alone and feeling very solitary, it is my only friend and comfort. Right, Pancho?"

Martín looked at Francisco but his brother was somewhere else. He stared back at Martín as though he had not heard a word and remained silent. Nick figured it was Barbarita he was brooding about or that he was worried about his daughter and thought it best to let him brood. But Martín had had enough.

"What's with you, Pancho? You've been preoccupied all evening."

"Sí."

"Then what is it? What's bothering you?"

Francisco looked from Martín to Nick then to his shot glass.

"I don't want to question what we're doing. But I'm worried. I don't understand what ought to happen."

Martín held his palms up and said, "When it happens we will know."

Nick said, "It bothers me, too, Pancho. I wish I had a better plan, a better idea what I want. But I can't let that stop me."

Nick paused and moved his eyes around the room as he thought how he wanted to say it. The room was large and square with wooden beams supporting a brick ceiling. The three men sat in the center of the room at a crude table—also square—that held two candles, the only light except for that coming from the fireplace. In front of the fireplace sat a heavy couch, constructed seemingly from surplus ceiling beams, with bulging leather cushions—horsehide, Nick presumed. On the brick wall over the fireplace hung a crucifix, a machete, and a calendar that bore a picture of Christ being carried in a sedan chair by Mexican bishops before a procession of lions, birds, and other wild beasts. In the far corner of the room sat a small kitchen—merely a sink with a hand pump, a bare wood counter top, and two gas burners. Near the kitchen a door led to a disused bedroom that Martín had insisted Nick take. Nick suspected that Martín was accustomed to sleeping on the couch in the glow of the fire. The floor of the house consisted of coarse stones cemented together and covered with woven Indian rugs. The room smelled smoky and good, and despite a strong wind blowing sand around outside, the fireplace drew well and the candles burned slowly. Nick continued:

"No, I don't know what will happen but I know that it is not yet time for me to leave. I'll watch Vicente's ranch and his fábrica. If my suspicions are correct, somehow he is obtaining true antiquities and selling them to collectors or smuggling them out of Mexico. I believe this is what my father learned and what caused his death. So I will see who comes and goes and then think about what I should do."

"But what can you do alone?"

"Perhaps I can discover something. Some evidence that would be valuable. I am not sure. But I must do something, Pancho."

Martín nodded. "Clearly."

Francisco shook his head. "Perhaps it is better to wait to see what Hernandez will do."

"Hernandez!" Martín said. "He cannot even protect Nicholas from Vicente's thugs. If Vicente does not want the father's body sent for further examination then it will not go—no matter what Hernandez does. Somewhere Vicente has powerful friends."

Francisco drank down his tequila and licked his lips.

"Which is another reason to be careful. To cross Don Vicente is to..."

"Fuck Don Vicente!" Nick barked. "He's only one man and I'm one man. I don't know what I'll do but I'll do something. It's no good trying to reason with me on this. I must understand my father's death. I have to see that he is buried properly just as you saw to Barbarita."

Francisco's head jerked back, he glared at Nick, and Nick wished he hadn't said it. But finally Francisco took in a breath and let it slowly out.

"Tienes razón. You are right. Forgive me. I am not accustomed to confronting those with power. It is in the blood."

"There is nothing to forgive. Besides, I don't plan to confront anyone, simply to observe. But I'm bothered also, Pancho. This is all new to me, this. . .this desire to know." Nick stared into his shot glass, turning it in his fingers.

"I never worried about anything or anyone. I always took what I wanted and did what I wanted—despite my father's advice. And of course the cabrón was always right. Now perhaps it is time for me to start listening to him, to heed what I hear him calling from the grave, to learn from his bones."

The wind blew sand against the windows and a log moved in the fireplace. Martín poured more tequila into the shot glasses and the three men drank together in silence.

■

When Alexander Petrov turned to write on the chalkboard, Nick slipped unnoticed into the back row of lecture hall chairs.

Rapt students, obediently recreating in their notebooks what their professor scrawled and intoned, surrounded him. Young for grad students, Nick thought, and innocent looking, though most were likely his own age.

Barely conscious of his father's droning voice he studied a blonde with smooth and seemingly supple legs seated just to his left in the row in front of him. He watched her write the words "TLALOC—RAIN GOD" in block letters, then "SORCERERS". She must have felt him staring for she glanced over her shoulder at Nick, who now focused his attention on his father.

Mysticism. Spiritual existence. How many lectures from his father had he endured, morning, noon, night? He wondered whether teaching made professors pedagogic or simply that natural pedants were drawn to the lectern.

Soon the sexy blonde was closing her notebook and standing, as were the other students. Nick rose and pushed down the aisle against the flow. When he was within ten feet of the stage his father looked up over the tops of semicircular reading glasses and focused on him.

Nick stopped just below the lectern and they stood silent, facing each other, his father looming over him.

"Is something wrong, Nicholas?"

Nick understood the question. Visits were that rare.

"No, nothing. Had to interview the new chancellor this morning for the

Sunday edition and thought I'd drop by for a few minutes."

Professor Petrov nodded, pursing his lips. "Coffee?"

Nick followed his father down a corridor and into the art and archeology department offices, where his father indicated a coffee maker behind the receptionist. Nick filled two cardboard cups with black coffee and shuffled down the hall with them to his father's office. There on shelves that covered three walls, clay and stone replicas of ancient ollas and figurines argued with books. Nick handed a cup to his father, who nodded at the chair across from him.

"And what does our esteemed chancellor have to say?"

Nick blew on the black liquid. "Onward and upward. Tradition and innovation. High standards and open admissions. Id est, crap."

The professor raised his eyebrows. "Is that how you'll write it?"

"I wish."

Nick looked away, as if studying the book titles on the shelf at eye level just to his right. He felt it beginning again, the unease, the sense of vulnerability. It was always as if he was defending a dissertation.

"You're bored already, aren't you, Son?"

Nick shrugged. "It'll get better. It's like being untenured. Someone has to teach the lower level courses. I'll get some clips here and move on. I've already started looking."

"Where?"

"Somewhere warm. I've had offers. Nothing any better though."

"Nothing to chew on?"

Nick shook his head. "Not yet. But it'll come."

"You need some substantial work, Nicholas."

"I know that. That's why I'm looking."

"Somewhere warm."

"Right."

His father took out his pipe and played at filling it.

"Have you saved any money?"

"Some."

"Good. I have a great investment opportunity for you. . ."

Nick opened his mouth in surprise as his father went on:

"Quit your job and come to Mexico with me this summer. Work the dig with me, document it, sell it to a magazine."

"Not much return on my money."

The senior Petrov put a match to his pipe.

"I wasn't talking about a financial return. . .When was the last time you went with me? Five, six years ago, after you were discharged, right? When will you have another chance? I tell you, there's magic at this new site. You can feel it in the air, in the jungle, in the people. Living with them is like stepping back a thousand years, and all that's modern and ephemeral falls away from you like dead skin from a molting snake. . .Speaking of snakes, last summer one of my workers there captured a poisonous jungle snake that is perfectly blind, navigating with heat sensors. I'd never seen such a thing..."

His father went on, off again on another lecture that would end in some other place, somewhere far away. Nick glanced surreptitiously at his watch thinking that if the blonde with the great legs was going on the dig as well, he might actually consider it.

Fourteen

Both Martín and Francisco were up at first light. But half awake, Nick heard them stirring about then slipped back into sleep.

He dreamt of being pursued by two dark, faceless men with machetes. They chased him down narrow streets, their footsteps sounding at his heels. But then Nick somehow pulled away from them, ducked around a corner, and hid in a doorway. He waited but heard nothing. So he peered around the corner to verify that they had gone. And the machetes fell, hacking into his shoulders, as the two dark men laughed. Nick woke sweating and heard what sounded like Martín's truck pulling away.

He waited for his heart to slow, knowing the adrenaline would dissipate in a few minutes. The same dream had harried him now for too many years—ever since he had settled into his life with Regan and become what he had become—and only the weapons changed. Now it was machetes instead of bayonets. After a while he was able to get back to sleep.

The day shone bright by the time he rose. At the kitchen pump Nick ran cold water over his head then boiled some for coffee and some extra to fill a goatskin bota Martín had loaned him. He scrambled eggs with onions, heated tortillas in the skillet, and ate at the square table.

Nick wrapped cold tortillas and a round of white ranch cheese in newspaper and tucked the package inside his shirt. He strung the bota over his shoulder, took the machete from the wall, and grabbed the binoculars from the table where Martín had left them.

Tethered to the corral fence he found the chestnut mare saddled and waiting. On the saddle horn Martín had tied a wide-brimmed straw hat. Nick tried the hat, removed it, and combed back his hair with his fingers. Then he pressed the hat low on his forehead and slung the binoculars, bota, and machete over the horn. He mounted the mare mindful of his tender ribs and urged the horse up the arroyo.

Moving up the path alongside the creek in the morning sun seemed to clear his head and brighten him. He had been dwelling too much on death—his father's, Barbarita's, even his own. Death had a palpable daily presence in Mexico. Miquitzli, panteones, pyramids. Dead, inert rock and lifeless sand. Even the houses, made of indestructible stone instead of wood, gave off a cool, tomb-like feel. A hard country.

But the feeling of death also came because time had stopped. Here he had lost autumn as he knew it: low, gray skies; cold, clear rain; the bite of damp wind. They called this high country The Land of Eternal Spring, and to him eternity meant only death.

And then there was Malena also contributing to his funereal mood. An American woman would have talked of living together, not dying together. No, if he had been dwelling too much on death it wasn't entirely his fault.

He heard bleating and looked up to see goats grazing on the sparse greenery that followed the creek up the ravine. A goatherd squatted in the shade of a tall cactus. When the old man saw Nick on horseback, he shifted his machete from his right hand to his left and touched the brim of his sombrero. Nick saluted likewise.

Nick pushed the horse upstream, hearing the sound of the waterfall growing. The ravine cut to the left, the noise increased, and he saw the cascading water. He guided the mare to the path that wound up

167

the side of the arroyo. At the top the horse lumbered across the mesa in the direction of the tall chain fence and Vicente's ranch. Again Nick saw in the distance the crucifix atop the Church of the Inquisition and again it seemed ethereal and unreal, like some purported vision of divinity.

When he saw the mesquite tree where they had rested previously and the fence and hacienda beyond it, Nick pulled on the reins and turned the horse around. He rode down into a gully, dismounted, and tied the mare to the trunk of a sabino tree. After taking the binoculars, bota, and machete from the saddle Nick walked back up the hill toward the fence and sat on the ground, leaning against a tall pine tree there. He pulled the binoculars from their case.

Focusing them he saw beside the stable the blue truck that had delivered the crate to the train station and, parked next to the house, a black jeep wagon. But he saw no activity, no people. Nick looked at his watch. Nine o'clock. It would be a long day, and he wondered if there was any point to this at all. Yes there was, he reminded himself, even if he learned nothing new. He would have tried.

Now he studied the house more carefully. To the left was a sala with glass-and-wrought-iron doors lining two sides. With the doors open as they now were, the room became an airy covered patio. A large fireplace on the right wall had deep chairs positioned in a semicircle around it. In front of the chairs sat a coffee table with magazines on it, and against the back wall stood a wooden cabinet with glass doors. Under a wrought-iron chandelier near the center of the room a small bar held variously colored bottles. To the left of the bar was a sofa and behind it a credenza on which rested a telephone, a lamp, and a vase like those in the crate at Vicente's shop. A woman entered the room carrying a bucket and mop.

Nick could see that her hair was pulled back from her face and braided in a long tail that hung nearly to her waist. She knelt and rolled up a carpet lying in front of the fireplace, standing it against the wall. Then she returned to her mop. Nick heard a fluttering above him and lowered the binoculars.

In the top of the pine tree sat a vermilion flycatcher. Putting the binoculars on it he saw a bright red crown and breast; the back, tail, and ear patches were blackish. It sang, "Pit-a-zee, pit-a-zee," then flew off, and Nick went back to watching the woman mop the floor.

At ten o'clock Vicente came into the room wearing a maroon bathrobe and carrying a newspaper and coffee cup, and sat in one of the chairs by the fireplace. Soon a second woman entered—this one in a white apron—and faced Vicente. He spoke to her briefly and she left the room. Ten minutes later she returned carrying a tray that she set on the coffee table in front of him and again disappeared.

Vicente read the newspaper as he ate. At ten-forty-five he got up and exited the room. At eleven Vicente reappeared at the front door of the house dressed in dark slacks and white shirt, got into the black station wagon, and drove off.

That was all Nick saw that morning.

At noon five men filed out of the fábrica behind the house and seemed to disappear into a back door of the hacienda. At twelve-thirty they returned to the factory and Nick unwrapped the package of tortillas and cheese.

When he was almost finished eating he looked up and saw a campesino driving a burro with packs tied to its back, prodding the animal up the drive toward the hacienda. Nick picked up the binoculars and trained them on the man. He had seen aged campesinos just like him in town trying to sell soil, nuts, firewood, or whatever else they could scavenge from the hard, dry earth.

The campesino rang the bell at the front door, which soon opened to reveal the woman who mopped the floor. The campesino appeared to speak and the woman shook her head. She exchanged a few words with the man and closed the door. He turned and drove the burro back down the drive.

At two-fifteen, the black station wagon returned. Vicente got out and disappeared into the house. Nick watched until two-thirty then let his eyes close.

The remainder of the afternoon proved hardly more eventful. At four o'clock Luis and Miguel showed up in a dusty white sedan and went into the house, each carrying a small parcel. At four-thirty the workers came out of the fábrica and pulled themselves up into the back of the blue truck. Luis or Miguel came out the front door of the hacienda followed by the cook and housemaid. The three climbed into the cab of the truck and off it drove. Nick spotted an Inca dove, a vulture, and a brown snake moving along the fence.

Within an hour the blue truck returned and the driver went inside the house. At six Nick saw Vicente and his two men enter the living room. One of the men went to the bar to mix drinks, and the three of them sat talking and smoking cigarettes in the cushioned chairs around the cold fireplace.

Nick waited until the sun hung low in the sky behind him before rising and making his way back down the hill to the sabino tree. The three men still sat in front of the fireplace, one or another occasionally rising to refresh the drinks.

Mounting the horse made Nick grit his teeth. After sitting against the tree for hours his ribs seemed to hurt more than the day before. His only exercise all day had been killing red ants with the machete before they could climb onto his ankles.

As he rounded the lake at the mouth of the arroyo, he saw Martín sitting on the running board of his truck turning a small goat on a spit over a wood fire. When Martín noticed Nick riding up he waved a beer bottle at him.

Nick unsaddled the mare, carried the binoculars, bota, and machete inside the house, and grabbed a beer from the ice chest beneath the sink. He went out through the screen door letting it slam behind him and leaned against the fender of the truck.

"I don't believe I could be a successful goatherd. What does one think about all day alone in the campo?"

"Women."

"I'll try that tomorrow. Today I watched Vicente's rancho for ten hours. Nothing happened. At ten-fifteen he has breakfast served to him on a tray in the living room. At eleven he goes to town for a few hours and returns home in time for comida and siesta. At six o'clock one of his jotos makes cocktails as Vicente relaxes in a cushioned chair by the fireplace. This is Vicente's day—while his workers are busy in the fábrica producing his wares and his servants clean and cook for him. Such is the life of the rich."

"You learned nothing then?"

Nick shook his head. "Perhaps something of the routine. It all seems innocent. He has a house with servants and a factory with workers. He runs a business. . .Perhaps Pancho was right. This seems a waste of time."

"But you are satisfying yourself."

"There is that. And I will get satisfied very quickly with any more days like this. I wonder what I expected to see."

Martín sliced off a piece of the roast cabrito and held it out to Nick on the tip of the knife.

"Try again tomorrow, Nicholas. Perhaps you will see the fat bastard with the lost treasure of Moctezuma. Then we will steal it and be rich too."

Nick took the piece of goat from the knife and talked as he chewed.

"Chinga a los ricos! I need another beer to wash the taste of boredom from my mouth."

And he went into the house to pull two more bottles from the cooler.

■

"Why did you say that in front of her—'She was a lady'—as if Regan wasn't?"

"I think you understand perfectly, Nicholas."

"I understand that she's not the same as my mother. Is that what you expected? For me to marry someone from the past?"

His father fell silent as if stung. But soon his voice came back calm.

"No, Son, but I do expect something other than drunken vulgarity in a woman—particularly one who's had her advantages."

Nick paused, checking himself, staring into the receiver as though he could see his father there, grasping it in his fist as if ready to smash it into his desk top. He took a deep breath and brought the telephone back to his lips.

"She wasn't drunk, Father."

"Then you admit she's vulgar—and tactless. She went on asking about Maria long after I made it clear to her that it was a subject I wished to avoid."

Nick pursed his lips. The most difficult part about arguing with his father was that the old man always had his facts straight, even if he came to wrongheaded conclusions.

"She was just trying to be friendly, to draw you out."

"I do not wish to be 'drawn out'. I wish to have my privacy respected. This Megan. . ."

"Regan, Father. Her name is Regan."

"She will not be a good mother to your children."

"We're not thinking about children."

"Then what is this marriage about? I am too old-fashioned. Explain it to

me. You are already sharing a bed with her. Why do you now wish volun-
tarily to pay for the privilege? You are being naive, Nicholas."

"Thanks for the worldly advice."

His father again fell silent. Nick felt bad for saying it, but he'd asked for
it. Finally his father's voice rasped from the receiver.

"Because I have chosen a scholarly life you think I have not lived. There
you are again wrong, Nicholas. I have lived a full life, I have observed, and
I have also benefited from the experience of others. I know about women
because I am a man with his eyes open, a man who fell in love and married,
a man who has read great literature and great thinkers and great scientists.
You are so American, Nicholas. For you the bookcase is merely ornamental.
You attempt independence of thought by ignoring the accumulated wisdom
of all who have gone before you. You believe you can make your own rules
and bend nature to your whim. If you marry this woman you will be sorry.
Yes, she is beautiful and elegant. But there is more to a life together than
physical attraction. That will diminish soon enough. I hope you prove me
wrong, but that has never yet happened."

Nick felt as if he were suffocating. His father left him no space in which
to breathe. If only the old man would leave him alone. If only he could leave
his father alone. And he saw that they would continue on like this—locked in
an archetypal danse macabre, in a mutual strangle hold—until the arrogant
old bastard died.

Fifteen

The routine seemed just that. Nick looked at his watch: five-o-one p.m. He had risen with Martín and was at his post beneath the pine tree in time to see the workers and servants arrive at seven in a white bus. Then it was the same.

Vicente breakfasted at ten-fifteen and left at eleven. The factory workers took a half hour off at noon and Vicente arrived home in time for his afternoon meal. At four-thirty the workers and servants were taken away in the blue truck. The vermilion flycatcher returned.

Only once all day had Nick felt any sense of purpose: when he rode up the arroyo at daybreak. The sun had not yet risen high enough to throw light over the steep arroyo walls. Dew clung to the cactuses and he could see his horse's breath. Along the creek the air hung silent and cool and Nick felt an aura of expectancy encircling him. But whatever hopeful expectations he harbored in the optimism of morning had now been ground to ennui by the day's inactivity.

To pass the time he had tried thinking of women, as Martín had suggested. He thought of his wife and what would happen when he returned. Would the time apart cure or change anything? Or would she be the same woman and he the same man and his return merely a paying of respects to the corpse of their marriage and arranging for its burial? More death thoughts.

He thought too of Malena, and unlike thoughts of his wife these kept returning by their own volition throughout the day. What did

175

that signal? The allure of novelty, he told himself, sexual and cultural. In both regards she was exotic, like a hothouse flower. He saw her dancing and saw her in bed, tasted her smooth brown flesh and felt the tight pull of her vagina on him. But most of all he thought of her coming to him in the rain when he had presumably called her telepathically. Of her fatalistic attachment to him. And of her words when he left: "I will wait for you until death." There was that word again, esperar—to wait, or to hope. He wondered which she meant—and whether they weren't the same thing anyway. But whichever, something unspoken and unconscious made him feel more for her than he should have by all rights. The dancing and the perfume and the sexual excitement got a man's attention. But something else made it hard to leave: the raw and tacit feelings buried deep inside, the instinct that made you feel responsible for her and mated to her.

He took a drink of tepid water from the bota and looked again at his watch: seven minutes past five. No, not much point in all this. Maybe he had done all he could. Today was just like yesterday and no doubt like tomorrow. And now even the same campesino who visited the house yesterday was coming up the drive again with his laden burro. Nick picked up the binoculars.

Yes, the same old man. Only the time was different. Yesterday he had come earlier in the day, while Vicente was away. Now he was back. But why? If he was selling potting soil, peanuts, or firewood, the servants who ran the household could likely have taken care of him the previous day. Nick refocused the glasses.

Through the binoculars he watched the old campesino shuffle to the front door and ring the bell. One of Vicente's bodyguards opened the door shielding his eyes from the sun sinking behind Nick. After a few seconds he—Luis or Miguel—closed the door on the campesino. But the old man did not go away.

Soon the door opened again and Vicente stepped through it. The old man spoke to him; Vicente shrugged; the campesino went to the burro. There he untied the packs strapped to either side of the animal, lifted them off over its back, and laid them on the ground as Vicente approached. With his back to Nick the old man knelt to unwrap the cloth sacks as Vicente squatted and reached down.

All Nick could now see was the campesino's back and the top of Vicente's head as he examined whatever the sacks contained. But then Vicente tilted back his head, turned to the side, and held an object up to the falling sun, studying it and turning it in his hand. To Nick it looked four or five inches high, gray or beige in color. Vicente then lowered the object and said something to the old man, who stood raising his hands. As he did suddenly Nick could see what lay on the ground atop the sacks: figurines, a vase, pottery fragments.

Vicente also stood, pulling at his belt, as the old man doffed his sombrero, holding it in front of him with both hands as he spoke. They talked back and forth for long minutes until Vicente turned his head to call over his shoulder into the house. One of the twins appeared at the door. Vicente raised his chin to speak to him and the man went back into the house.

Vicente returned the artifacts to the sacks and carried them inside through the open doors of the sala. The bodyguard came back through the front door, counted out a stack of peso notes to the old man, and closed the door behind him as he re-entered the house.

Standing alone with his burro the old peasant recounted the money one bill at a time then did it again. Finally satisfied, he put the money in his hat, replaced the hat on his head, and led the burro back down the drive. Nick turned the glasses on the living room.

Vicente sat before the fireplace, his man beside him, once again removing the pieces from the sacks and placing them on the coffee table. Nick took another drink of boiled water from the bota.

At five-forty-five the blue truck came up the drive and stopped by the stable. The driver got out and joined the others in the living room. After examining the artifacts on the coffee table, he went to the bar and made drinks for the three of them. At six-twenty Vicente carried the pieces one by one to the glass cabinet against the back wall and locked them inside.

It was then that Nick moved back down the hill to the chestnut mare, mounted, and let her lope across the darkening mesa to the ravine.

Martín spread his hands palms up.

"That is no good either. It's the same everywhere.With Hernandez, with the military, with the government. Those who have power are not honest and those who are honest have no power. Without doubt Vicente has políticos in his pocket—perhaps in the governor's office, maybe in the capital. Surely Hernandez wishes to be rid of Don Vicente but can do nothing. He could lose his job—or worse."

Nick nodded slowly and stared at the table. Martín continued:

"Even if the authorities could act and catch Vicente with the artifacts he would pay someone to make his problems go away or the evidence disappear. No, when a man has power no one knows his secrets."

Martín struck a match and lit a candle on the table. The air turned from gray to amber. Nick peeled the yellow label from a beer bottle with his thumb.

"Then somehow we must expose his secrets."

"Como?"

Nick stared at the candle. Then he rose, moved to the bedroom, and returned carrying the book with the photo of the stone effigy on the cover. He laid it open on the table and pulled from it a clipping that he slid across the table to Martín. The Mexican bent over the newspaper article, his eyes scanning up and down, left and right.

"Es Vicente, sí?"

Nick nodded.

"What does it say?"

Martín handed the article back to Nick, who paraphrased from the English:

"Se dice que Vicente Villas fábrica buenas copias de antigüedades. And that these copies he makes are so good that they even fool museums. It says that his business is very successful and within the law but that he depends on people believing it is not."

Martín nodded. Nick looked up from the clipping.

"But now we have learned that his business is not within the law. That he also deals in true art treasures, which are the property of the Mexican people. I am sure this is what my father learned and what led to his death. . .Now if Vicente's patrons—those who are protecting him—were to read in the Mexico City newspapers that Vicente Villas is a thief who robs Mexico of her heritage, his power would disappear overnight."

Martín said, "Sí. I understand. But such a thing is impossible."

"No, it can be done. For example, I could present the artifacts to the Museum of Anthropology at Chapultepec in my father's name, then reveal to the newspapers and television that they came from a disreputable dealer, Vicente Villas."

"Truly? You could do this?"

"It is easy, more or less. In the United States people pay me to arrange such stories in the newspaper. Here I can hire people in the capital to do the same."

Martín looked at Nick, frowning. "It is a good idea, Nicholas, but...but you do not have the antiquities."

"No, I do not have the antiquities." Nick took a sip from his beer bottle. "If there had not been the problems between Vicente and me, I could have bought the artifacts from him. Perhaps we could find someone to buy them for me. . .There was another gringo at the hotel, a white-bearded man interested in antiquities. . .Or Malena. That might be better."

Martín sat silent for a moment before speaking.

"But how would you know you were getting the true antiquities that the campesino unearthed? We are not experts and this. . ." Martín picked up the newspaper article with Vicente's photo. "This says even experts can be fooled."

Nick looked at the Mexican then picked up his beer bottle. He drained it off, set it back down on the table, and silently peeled off more of the label with his thumb.

It seemed like he had lain awake half the night. He might have slept but he wasn't sure. Yet when he looked at his watch by moonlight coming through the bedroom window it was only eleven-thirty.

He could let it go, as Malena had pleaded. Go home, write some letters, and perhaps get some official action—although in Mexico that seemed less than likely. But so what if he couldn't find "justice"? What difference did it make? His father was dead. Gone. The corpse he sought to retrieve was not his father, just bones. An artifact. Where he was buried made no difference to the deceased—despite the waiting grave beside his departed wife. No difference at all—unless one believed in spiritual existence. Which Nick did not.

He shook his head imperceptibly at himself. Why couldn't he let it go? His whole life he'd been running from his father and what he represented. But now he found himself wishing to embrace his father in death—found himself questing for his bones as though they were his own, as though he needed them to stand.

But why? Was what his father represented now something he needed? The old man's world was one of belief—in traditions, in gods, in the power of blood. Where a man was his father's son. But even as a child Nick had perceived that all that was the Old World, to him a dead world. And that America was chaos, where all sorts mixed and bred, where fortunes were made and legacies lost and forgotten. A land where a disciplined intellect and a cautious adherence to form got you a walk-up flat and a window on the world going by. But that wasn't enough for Nick, thorough American that he was, incautious and crass, wasteful, at times violent. He applied his most precious inheritance—his Petrov intellect—to transient, mercantile concerns. Successfully, to his mind if not his father's. But now for some reason he felt compelled to act, compelled by the world he had scorned. A world of tradition and blood and spirit that now called to him as though an echo from a hollow place inside himself.

But maybe something more was at work in this: pride, as triggered by Vicente. I could kill the fat fuck, Nick thought. Unctuous son of a bitch. What did Vicente know about what happened to Nick's father—and what part did he play in it? To think of him getting away with it, getting away with everything. Nick once again saw Vicente grinding his prick against Malena on the dance floor, then saw him in bed with her, saw his prick going into her. . .

Nick sat up on the edge of his bed to clear his head. With no electricity there was no light to flip on—only a candle Martín had given him and the moonlight. Nick lifted a pack of cigarettes from the shirt hanging on a chair back and struck a match. He lit a cigarette and then the candle.

No wind tonight. Outside he heard vague rustlings and scratchings in the earth. He looked down at the stone floor and in the candlelight saw a small, brown scorpion inches from where he had placed his feet. Nick lifted his feet from the cool stones.

Was it the Olmecs? Or maybe the Toltecs. One of the tribes—maybe all of them—believed in totem animals. The first living creature you saw when you were born became your totem—whether a jaguar, a bird, a snake, or a cow—and you took on its characteristics. Maybe the same applied to waking, he thought. Maybe a man could take on the quiet and dangerous qualities of the scorpion.

Nick reached down to the floor for his shoes, shook them out, and slipped them on. He stood, pressed out his cigarette in an ashtray on the chair, and stepped heavily on the scorpion.

Martín was asleep on the couch. Nick carefully lifted the machete and binoculars from the hook above the fireplace, eased out the door without a sound, and made his way by moonlight to the corral.

■

The warm smell of the city wafted to him on a night breeze, a moist, fertile aroma of spring—the scent of rich ancient earth, of bricks still damp from an evening cloudburst, of wet bark and newspapers, of basil and rosemary and blooming lilac. Leaning back in a chair on his father's fire-escape landing, Nick sensed that it was one of those perfect May nights that once held such an aura of expectation for him—and of hope.

Surrounded by terracotta pots containing black earth and the early green shoots of spring, both he and his father sat with white shirtsleeves rolled to the elbow. Surreptitiously Nick glanced at his watch.

"Relax, Nicholas," said the old man. "Enjoy the evening. This may be our last time together for a long while. You know the Mexicans accuse us gringos of not living inside our bodies. Here is a chance to do just that. Breathe in the night air. Have some more vodka."

Without waiting for a reply his father reached over with the perspiring bottle and poured more clear liquor into Nick's shot glass resting on the wrought-iron cafe table. This on top of the Czech beer served with a supper of stuffed cabbage that, for some reason, his father had gone to some pains to prepare. Nick figured he'd have a bad head in the morning but wasn't quick enough to refuse and knew—as his father did—that once it was in his glass he would drink it. Rather odd, though, the old man pressing liquor on him given Nick's history with it and his father's disapproval of that history.

"What will you do with your summer, Nicholas?"

It was, Nick noticed, another version of the enduring—and as yet to be

183

satisfactorily answered—parental query, "What will you do with your life?" As usual Nick shrugged.

"Work. See a few ball games. Get some sun." As he said it he realized how insipid it must sound to his father.

"Any chance of your joining me at the dig for a week or two?"

Nick shook his head. "Sorry. No time. Regan and I are planning a trip to Paris. That's all the vacation I have left."

"I see."

The conversation, Nick saw, covered old ground: the end of the semester, his father's leaving for Mexico, an invitation to join him, Nick's polite refusal. And, of course, Nick's ill-formed plans for the future.

"It's not too late, Nicholas."

Nick stared at him. "Not too late for what?"

His father's eyes seemed to dart back and forth over Nick's face. The old man took a deep breath, chest heaving, and after a silence said:

"You know, Son, it's a good life. Despite whatever disappointments and regrets, despite whatever sorrows."

Nick nodded, his tongue pushing out his left cheek. That too was odd. A new twist on the standard conversation: vague philosophical pronouncements. Now Nick made a point of looking at his watch.

"Gotta get up early for a big meeting," he lied, pushing himself up from the metal chair.

His father pursed his lips and nodded as though in resignation.

"I'll walk you down."

"It's not necessary."

His father followed him down the front stairs and stood on the stoop as Nick moved across the red brick sidewalk to his car. Then as he eased the car from the curb something made Nick turn, and he saw his father standing under the electric light waving to him. An almost childlike wave, it seemed an excessively sentimental gesture for the old man.

As he steered the car down the block Nick glanced in the rearview mirror and saw his father still giving him the loose-wristed wave. Damn odd. Almost as if, Nick mused, he was saying his last goodbye.

Sixteen

Nick lowered the binoculars and looked to his watch. Midnight. Malena was no doubt dancing at La Última Cena—there was nowhere else to go in Escondido. Vicente was likely in attendance as well. Their lives back to normal. Again he trained the glasses on Vicente's hacienda—the house dark, the jeep wagon gone—then laid the binoculars aside.

Sitting on his haunches he stared through the hurricane fence, glanced again at his watch, and tapped a nervous rhythm on the hard ground with the machete. Okay, okay. A close look was all he needed. His father had taught him how to look at them and what to look for to be sure he'd know them later. Just a few minutes inside then out again. Easy.

But he still sat tapping the machete on the ground, not moving, telling himself this was a damn lot easier than going out on ambush in the dark Vietnamese night, always looking over your shoulder for fear that Charlie was there waiting to turn the ambusher into the ambushee. Okay. He lifted the machete higher and thrust it into the sandy earth. Then again. And he began pulling the broken earth from beneath the fence with his hands.

After a few minutes of digging he then used the blade of the machete to measure the width and depth of the furrow he had dug, then dug some more. When he was satisfied he paused and took another look at the house.

No lights on inside, no movement. The sala was in a good spot if Vicente came home while he was inside. He could spot any headlights coming up the road long before he could be seen, then escape in the dark on the far side of the house. Nick took a deep breath, lay on his back, and began walking his shoulder blades through the opening below the fence, clutching the machete to his chest.

Once through the fence he rolled to his knees and again eyed the hacienda. All was dark except for a yellow outside lamp near the front door and another—a night light, seemingly—glowing from the factory behind the house. But it was a clear night and the moon looked a perfect half so he had plenty light to see where he was walking.

Crouching, he moved on a straight line toward the left corner of the hacienda. He heard an owl hoo-hooing but perceived no further sound other than the scuffling of his tennis shoes over the sand and pebbles.

Cuídate. That's what everyone told him. Take care of yourself. Y tranquilo, Nick. Calm. Calm and careful. He had always acted calmly back then, even when his insides churned hot and he yearned to bolt. And he had always been careful, almost always, and everything worked out okay. He had made it back in one screwed-and-glued piece when a lot of other guys hadn't. But now he had that same feeling he had had then when he was appearing so calm and acting so careful, the feeling that it wasn't happening to him but to some other poor bastard who had borrowed his body for the night. In those days he saw everything he did as though a newsreel of his life. If the V.C. he was trying to talk out of a tunnel had flipped up a grenade or popped up from another rat hole behind him shooting, Nick surely would have acted decisively and without panic, but only because of the feeling that he wasn't personally involved.

It was too otherworldly and surrealistic for him not to feel detached. He had been expected to reason with the enemy after his comrades had rolled concussion grenades into the tunnel—just to get their attention, seemingly, though a hell of a way to start a conversation. He had thought what it must be like for them, the men cornered in the tunnel with grenades rolling toward them, and at night he even dreamed about it. Nick also remembered walking on the balls of his feet the whole time, ready to jump this way or that, and recalled an incessant vibration in his chest that, in those days, never went away, not even when he slept. He had thought then that it was healthy fear, telling him he shouldn't be where he was doing the things he was doing, and now he felt it again.

The house wasn't far—two hundred yards he figured—but there was nowhere to hide if a car came up the road now. No bushes, no trees, no gullies. Just a long even slope down to the house and it seemed like forever before he reached it.

He leaned against the cool stucco wall of the hacienda under the eaves, listening, hearing only his own heart pounding in his ears and his own breath. He waited, letting his heart slow, trying to relax. But after a minute and a half he realized that the vibration in his chest wasn't going away and decided to get on with it.

He tried the lever handles of the leaded glass doors on the front of the house—where Vicente had entered earlier—without success. Then he moved along the left side of the hacienda and checked the doors there. Locked as well.

He figured he could break a pane of glass and reach in to unlock the door, but didn't want Vicente to know anyone had been there if he could help it. Nick pushed where the two glass doors came together and felt them move a bit. With a little luck maybe he could spring them open. He slid the tip of the machete beneath the metal lip where the twin doors met and tugged. They gave somewhat but not enough.

He got a better purchase with the machete by turning it vertical, the handle at the top and the length of the blade beneath the metal lip. He grabbed the wooden handle of the machete with both fists and tugged. The doors moved in an inch then returned to their original position. He pulled harder. Nick heard a crack and the doors sprung open, swinging inward. He stopped the left one with his free hand but the right swung beyond his reach, hitting the corner of a low table just inside. A pane cracked, fell from its frame, and shattered on the stone floor of the sala, the horrible sound reverberating throughout the long, stone room and seemingly throughout the house.

He stood perfectly still, not breathing, waiting—hoping. But when the sound died, nothing replaced it except for the hooting of the owl. He stepped through the opened doors into the moonlit living room.

Nick went directly to the wood-and-glass cabinet to his left, on the back wall, where he had seen Vicente place the artifacts. There were no handles on the cabinet doors, only a brass fitting for a skeleton key. He placed the tip of the machete blade between the doors at the lock and gently pried them open. After tucking the machete under his left arm Nick struck a match.

What he had seen only as vague shapes through the binoculars now became distinct and definable. A vase painted with black and white images of eyes and faces; a large stone figurine of a dancer; and smaller figures of gods, seemingly.

The vase would be easy to recognize anywhere, a beautiful piece, nearly unmarred. Where did the campesino find it? How much would Vicente want for it? Nick set the machete on top of the cabinet and reached for the vase. As he did, the lamp atop the credenza behind him burst on.

Nick whirled with that feeling of a grenade rolling toward him and saw Vicente at the doorway by the fireplace, one hand at the light switch on the wall, the other grasping a small, nickel-plated automatic. Nick backed away from the cabinet on the balls of his feet.

Vicente did not smile nor speak. The gun shone in the soft lamp light as though it radiated energy from its own center, and looked tiny and lost in Vicente's thick hand.

Nick suppressed an urge to turn and run into the night through the open doors behind him. Tranquilo. At that range he was a big target and hard to miss. His eyes fixed on the dark hole of the gun barrel.

Or Vicente could shoot him where he now stood if he wished, and bury him in the campo without anyone ever knowing. Or shoot him and call Police Chief Hernandez to take the intruder's body to the Petrov family plot at the panteón.

Nick edged backwards toward the open door to put some distance between him and the gun barrel and thus make a successful shot less likely if he summoned the nerve to run for it—and if Vicente had the guts to shoot.

"Sit down. Stop now and sit."

As Vicente clamped his jaw tight his jowls filled out, and Nick could see his fat neck pulsing and his hate-filled eyes boring into the gringo. He looked ready enough to pull the trigger. Nick inched to his right—past the credenza to the sofa Vicente had indicated with the pistol—and leaned against the sofa back, half sitting. Vicente stepped closer.

"Lift your hands."

Nick raised his hands. Vicente grabbed the machete from atop the cabinet and with the flat of the blade slapped Nick's sides, thighs, and back. Vicente looked satisfied that he was unarmed and Nick lowered his hands.

Vicente ordered: "Tell me who you are."

Nick sat without expression, figuring what to say, if anything, while his eyes noted every detail. After only a few seconds the scene seemed burned into his brain. He could have shut his eyes and described perfectly the rings on Vicente's fingers, the folds in his camel-colored sweater, the spatial relationship between Vicente's hulking outline and the backdrop of fireplace, chairs, and carpets. But he said nothing.

Vicente nodded slowly but spoke quickly, flatly, "Are you from the gringos?"

Meaning the U.S. government, Nick assumed. Vicente didn't realize that he was the son of the dead professor—apparently Hernandez hadn't told him. Vicente did not know that he was no one, just a man searching for his father's bones as though they might augur an alterable future for him or bestow upon him a boon with which to return home. And this is what his willful and quixotic venture—not his first—got him: Mexican jail time or perhaps even death. No, he was not from the government, had no influence, no highly placed friends, no power. But telling Vicente the whole truth would likely make it worse. Nick shook his head.

"No. I am not from the government."

Anyway, it probably made no difference what he said. For whatever reasons he had come seemingly to steal art treasures that Vicente possessed illegally. And he realized that Vicente's unlawful possession of the artifacts might make it difficult for him to turn Nick over to the police for attempting to steal them. The vibration in Nick's chest intensified and his ears began to hum.

"What are you doing in Escondido?"

When Nick did not answer, Vicente tried another question.

"What were you looking for?"

Again Vicente awaited an answer that did not come. Then he moved to the telephone on the credenza, picked up the receiver with his left hand, and laid it beside the phone. He dialed five digits and retrieved the receiver, keeping the gun in his right hand pointed at Nick's chest.

"Andrés? Sí. Están allí Miguel y Luis? Do you know where they went? It is important that you find them. Go to La Última Cena. They are probably there. Have them come to the rancho immediately. Tell them it is urgent and call me as soon as you find them." He hung up the phone and moved to his right, away from the credenza.

Nick could feel the dampness in his palms against the sofa back. Vicente had not called Hernandez to come arrest the interloper. Instead he had called the two men who fetched his drinks, carried his packages, and exacted his vengeance. Nick could see Vicente's nostrils flaring. Finally the Mexican blurted out:

"You are a very stupid gringo. Even more stupid than most. You come to my town and act as though it is yours. You interfere where you do not belong and where you know nothing. You insult me and smile. You take the woman who...this Malinche...and soil her forever. You and your blue eyes and your piggish American stupidity."

So that. Malena. Not the amulet nor his illegal business nor the fight, but the woman. And now Nick saw that he might die because of her. Vicente was right. He was stupid. He had come for one thing and let another—along with a deep-buried anger—ruin it. Now his father would lie forever in the dry, white earth. Or, more likely, have his bones turned out in the trash with the broken Coke bottles, banana peels, and toilet paper. And perhaps the same would happen to the son.

They waited without either saying a word. Minutes passed, long minutes. Nick felt a light breeze from the open door behind him. He could run—Vicente would either shoot him in the back or, less likely, fail to pull the trigger. Or Nick could wait for Luis and Miguel, who had already assaulted him twice, to return. Maybe they would decide to turn him over to Hernandez after all. But Nick had a feeling that wasn't going to happen.

The telephone rang. Vicente looked at it and moved toward the credenza. As he did Nick sprang forward, pushing off the sofa with his arms and legs and diving headfirst at Vicente. The gun fired and Nick's left ear went deaf as his hip struck the credenza. It went over with the lamp, telephone, and terracotta jug. The lamp popped and everything went dark as Nick's head struck beneath Vicente's chin. The big man stumbled backward and hit hard on the stone floor with Nick on top of him.

In the sudden darkness Nick grabbed for Vicente's hand where the gun lay wrapped tight in a death grip, his finger still on the trigger. Vicente tried to turn it toward him. Nick smelled Vicente's cologne and the tobacco on his warm breath. Bearing down with his weight behind him, Nick held Vicente's gun hand to the floor while raising his own right fist then dropping it. The blow glanced off Vicente's cheekbone, scraping knuckles on the stone floor. With Nick momentarily off balance, Vicente raised the gun from the floor, struggling to point it into Nick's deaf ear and his brain.

Nick felt his fingertips brush something hard that slid away from him. He reached out again with his right and found the clay vase that had sat on the credenza. Now this he lifted with his right arm and let fall in his fist and this time it was no glancing blow. He heard a cracking and thought it was the vase. But as his eyes adjusted to the dim, reflected moonlight he saw blood pouring from Vicente's flattened nose and running into the fat man's eyes. However, the Mexican still gripped the automatic, striving still to turn it on Nick. The gun suddenly jerked as Vicente squeezed off a second round, whose heat and concussion Nick felt on his face as it whizzed by.

Nick pressed down on Vicente's right wrist, above which the gun lay gripped, leaning into it and at the same time again raising and dropping the vase. Vicente moved to ward off the blow with his left arm but Nick's right was stronger. He brought the vase down against the side of his head and Vicente let out a bovine-like groan.

Nick lifted the vase—now mottled a deep, moonlit red on its underside—and let it fall again. Se cayó. It fell itself, as the Mexicans say, taking no personal responsibility for the broken cup or the spilled milk. Se cayó. Nick watched this newsreel from the last row of the balcony as the vase kept falling all by itself.

The gun now lay on the floor beside Vicente's limp hand. However, Nick saw himself once again raise the vase over his head as if to strike yet another blow. But bright, sudden light caught him and froze him as though in a candid color snapshot—arrested movement, a look of surprise, bright reds.

A car whose approach had been muffled by the ringing in his ears skidded to a halt outside, its front bumper almost crashing into the glass-and-wrought-iron doors of the sala. In the bright, painful light of its headlamps Nick saw the bloodied vase in his hand, gazing at it as though wondering how it got there. His eyes followed a trail of splattered blood from the vase down his arm to the front of his shirt to the gelatinous red face of Don Vicente. The vase dropped from his hand, cracking open on the stone floor. A voice called as if from afar, a vague, indecipherable noise in his right ear. He saw Vicente's pistol lying on the floor before him and as he dove for it a boot kicked it away.

He looked up. Chief of Police Hernandez stood over him, Martín at his side.

"The lights," Hernandez said, shielding his eyes from the glare of the auto's headlamps.

Martín found the switch that fired the wrought-iron chandelier at the center of the room then rushed outside to kill the car lights. The police chief pushed his cap back on his head and gazed down at Vicente Villas.

Nick followed his stare. Vicente's eyes, ringed with blood, gaped back immobile and unblinking. And he wished now that he had told Vicente why he had come to Escondido, so Vicente would know that Nick had taken his vengeance.

Hernandez seemed to make a move toward Nick, who drew back. But instead the chief reached down and retrieved from the floor a bloody fragment of the shattered vase that had killed Vicente. He frowned at it, lifted it to his nose to sniff, then held it out to Nick.

Nick reached for the shard gingerly, taking it between fingertip and thumb as though contaminated. He stared at it and frowned. Between the base and inner wall he saw a hollow portion filled with black paste. He too sniffed it and detected a vinegary aroma. When he handed it to Martín, who now stood huffing beside the chief, the ranchero studied it, shrugged, and looked to Hernandez.

"Caballo negro," said Hernandez. "Black horse heroin." Then he laid his hand on Martín's shoulder. "Go to Vicente's stable, amigo, and see if you can find a shovel."

As they were preparing to place Vicente on the rug that had lain in front of the fireplace, Nick kicked aside the broken lamp and telephone that had fallen from the credenza and remembered Vicente's phone call to Andrés. He turned to Hernandez.

"They're coming. Los dos, Luis y Miguel."

Hernandez moved his head from side to side.

"When Martín came and told me what was happening I sent a man to find them. I did not want those snakes coming up and biting me on the ass. They are in the can by now. Tomorrow I will present them to the commandant of the drug exercise with my evidence."

Martín and Nick loaded the rug into the trunk of the police car and put the room in order while Hernandez searched the house and fábrica.

As Hernandez drove the car across the dark, hard terrain Martín explained to Nick:

"I heard you riding off and followed. I arrived in time to see you moving down the hill toward the hacienda. Then I saw the light go off in the fábrica. But before I could get beneath the fence, there was Vicente in the sala with his pistol. All I could think to do was to get help. So I rode like hell straight to town, to Chief Hernandez's house, and prayed we would not be too late."

"Gracias, amigo. Y gracias a Dios," Nick muttered.

Hernandez selected a site near a dried creek bed half a kilometer from the house. Martín and Nick took turns digging, working by moonlight. Though the earth was not as hard as the high ground they encountered numerous rocks, some so large it took the strength of both men to lift them aside. Martín and Nick now hefted yet another bulky stone from the grave and rolled it onto the mound of dirt beside the opening in the earth. As Martín pulled himself from the hole Nick resumed digging.

Hernandez sat on the back bumper of the police car, watching; behind him in the open trunk lay the rug with Vicente rolled up inside. As Nick pushed the spade into the earth with his foot, scraping it through the rocky soil, he saw the policeman staring at the ground between his feet and chuckling to himself.

"What are you laughing at?"

Shaking his head Hernandez said, "God moves in mysterious ways. With patience, justice comes."

"Have you waited long?"

"Sí. For a long time. I could do nothing—and could not help you— because Vicente was protected. But a dead man cannot pay bribes. Certainly the drug commandant will be disappointed."

"What will you tell him?"

"That Vicente Villas has gone into hiding in Cuba after learning the gringo drug agents were onto him and would soon alert our government—an event that would have been very embarrassing to the comandante: the public denouncement of a narcotraficante operating under his nose. Now, however, with the package of heroin I found in the factory the general can demonstrate his efficiency to his superiors."

Hernandez stood and lifted his chin toward the deepening hole.

"It is better this way. For everyone. The general is once again an honest man, I again control my own town. And you, Petrov, walk away free and avenged. Yes, this is best. Very clean, very elegant."

An image of Vicente's bloodied face came to Nick's mind as he thrust the spade back into the ground. He lifted more dirt and threw it over his shoulder.

"Enough," said Hernandez. "Come out of the hole and put in the fat man."

Nick pulled himself from the grave and moved with Martín to the car as Hernandez stepped aside. Each grabbed an end of the rolled carpet, looked to the other, and heaved. Nick saw in Martín's eyes that he remembered too: This wasn't the first corpse they had lifted together.

They scraped Vicente's wrapped body over the lip of the trunk and set it on the ground. Then they both grabbed the end nearest the grave and dragged Vicente to its edge. Martín stepped back from the body and looked to Nick.

"Si quieres. . .If you wish, Nicholas, it is for you to do."

Standing over the bulging rug Nick wiped his hands on his bloodied shirt then stooped to grasp the edge of the carpet. He pulled but it unrolled only a few inches. So he pushed on the body with his foot to help it along. Vicente turned and out rolled his corpse, falling heavily into the grave.

Nick stood over him staring at the blood-caked face, at the camel-colored sweater now splotched red, at the length of him lying still in the earth. Then suddenly Nick let loose the carpet and leapt into the grave.

"Nicholas!"

Martín raced forward to the grave's edge with Hernandez beside him. They stared wide-eyed into it, where Nick knelt on the dead man's chest, hands at Vicente's throat. Martín dropped to his knees and reached down into the grave to lay a hand on Nick's shoulder.

"What are you doing, Nicholas? Come and let him rest."

Nick leaned back, taking his hands from Vicente's neck but then raising his right fist in the air as if to pummel the bloody corpse. The two Mexicans gasped in unison, gaping speechless at the mad gringo. But instead of punishing the dead man further Nick turned with his upraised fist held out to Martín and Hernandez and said, "Kukulcan."

The three men silently stared at the jade amulet dangling in moonlight from the leather thong in Nick's fist, admiring the ancient carving of the plumed serpent, the image of the snake-god that can fly.

■

No, this was not what Nick had come for, not what he had expected to find among his father's effects. He had hoped for a glimpse of some telling crack in his father's steely countenance, for a voyeuristic peek under his impenetrable armor. But he had not anticipated this, to be uncovering not his father's past but his own.

He looked up from the letter written in his own hand trying to see himself as he was then at eighteen, gung-ho boot camp volunteer, and felt a deep sense of loss, not only of his father but of time. How much of his life he had wasted. How many of his efforts had been misdirected, neurotic.

Nick lowered his eyes once more to the letter, shaking his head. How apparent it was now at twenty years' distance what a fool he had been. So eager to establish his manhood, so driven to wrest independence from what he saw as his overbearing father that he would even risk his life to achieve it. The grand gesture. How histrionic and stupid. And so painfully apparent in his written words—the words not of a man but of a boy masquerading as a man. Words that his father—who did nothing without good reason—had saved all these years. And Nick saw that even from the grave his old man continued to lecture him.

And more archival surprises. Neatly bound in rubber bands every letter Nick had written him from Nam. And newspaper clippings: "Petrov Passes Crusaders Over Toothless Tigers", "Petrov Scores In Nick Of Time, Leads Corpus Christi To City Title", "Petrov Awarded Purple Heart"; plus his first by-lined articles on local politics and groundbreakings—the insipid Americana that his father disdained but here preserved like rare artifacts illuminating a buried past. New, albeit circumstantial, evidence on the dead archeologist, forcing Nick to re-evaluate long-held theories. Was it possible that the old man actually took some sort of pride in his son's misguided actions?

But more disturbing and surprising—though, as Nick pondered it, it seemed almost predictable—was what he didn't find: nothing personal and revealing. No love letters, no diaries, no sentimental souvenirs nor old clothes too beloved to throw away. Other than the shoe box with Nick's letters and clips, nothing that might say this was a man's home for thirty-five years and not merely a stage set for a drawing-room farce. One small closet of clothes, the good china of his long-dead wife, a wooden box containing a screwdriver, a hammer, and pliers.

The only thing that may have given any clue to the secret longings of Alexander Joseph Petrov, Ph.D., was the professor's library. But even here the books were so eclectic it would have been hard for a stranger to draw valid conclusions. A bit heavy, naturally, on the pre-Columbian history and archeology. Literature scattered from Homer to Henry Miller, from Milton to Czeslaw Milosz; large doses of philosophy running from Aristotle to Nietzsche; travel guides from around the world; Marx, John Stuart Mill, C. Wright Mills, Montaigne, arranged alphabetically in a socio-political section

Nick suspected that sorting through his father's belongings at his campus office would yield similar results. The crafty archeologist knew only too well what sorts of conclusions people drew from the artifacts of the dead and so had arranged to frustrate any domestic autopsy. But had he always lived this way, as if ready to die? Apparently, Nick told himself, since death came so suddenly and unexpectedly. A cautious man. A disciplined man. An enigma.

All Nick had found was a discomfiting mirror held up to his own life. And he looked down again to the sophomoric letter in his hand, trying to grasp what had happened to the years since he wrote it.

Seventeen

Nick squatted in the shade of a lone cottonwood tree; Hernandez stood leaning against the trunk. Nick reached again into his left shirt pocket for the pack of cigarettes, put the last one between his lips, and threw the crumpled pack to the ground. He found matches in the other shirt pocket, lit the cigarette, and went back to watching the head of the grizzled old gravedigger disappear and reappear behind the mound of dirt, to which he now added another spadeful of earth. On the ground next to the deepening hole lay the crude wooden cross with "Petrov" hand-lettered across it.

Hernandez looked up the hill to his right and after staring there for a moment said, "What did you tell her?"

Nick also turned his head to gaze at Malena, who knelt beside her own father's shaded grave at the top of the hill. "Only that the bad blood between Vicente and me is finished. She saw the Kukulcan around my neck but asked no questions."

"That's typical. Soon she will hear the gossip—the story of Don Vicente's escape—and pretend to accept it as truth despite the re-appearance of the amulet. Later she will come to believe it herself. She is very Mexican."

Nick studied her. The black dress, the smooth bronze face, the Mayan profile. Very Mexican. Hernandez used the exact phrase to describe Malena that she had used for her father. Nick lifted his chin toward her and the shaded crypt.

"Did you know her father?"

"The general? Yes, I knew him. First commandant of the drug soldiers."

He said it flatly, which made Nick look up at Hernandez.

"What sort of man was he?"

Hernandez returned Nick's gaze with a raised eyebrow, hesitated a moment, then swept his hand palm down across the horizon, as though circumscribing the cemetery.

"They used to call this Escorza's bone yard."

Nick took a pull on his cigarette and shook his head as he stared at Malena beside her father. "Now it truly is."

There came a sound like someone knocking on a door and both men looked toward the gravedigger. Nick rose throwing his cigarette butt to the ground with the others he'd smoked and strode toward the grave. Hernandez followed.

The old gravedigger worked faster now. He scraped away the earth from one end of the wooden coffin, turned around, and lifted final spades of dirt from the other.

As Nick stood above the gravedigger he saw Malena coming down the hill, the skirt of the black dress swinging from side to side as she walked. She approached and stopped at the other end of the grave.

The old man dug out around the soiled pine box, slid thick ropes over either end, and with the aid of a crowbar worked them underneath. The sun beat down on Nick's forehead but he saw no perspiration on the gravedigger's face. Soon the ropes were in place.

"Now I will get help for the lifting," he said and started to climb from the grave.

"Momentito," said Nick.

The others looked at him.

"Open it."

Nick stood with arms folded across his chest, staring at the coffin. He had seen enough of Mexico to know that to endure here one had to take virtually everything on faith—but he himself possessed little of the commodity.

Hernandez looked from Nick to the crowbar lying on the mound of dirt. He stooped to retrieve it and handed it down to the gravedigger.

The old man balanced himself with legs spread, feet planted in the dirt on either side of the coffin. He hooked the curved end of the tool under a corner of the lid and yanked. There came a cracking sound and he yanked again. Then he rotated the crowbar in his hands and beat down on the edge of the coffin lid until the tops of nails rose from the wood. Now he was able to slide the other, beveled end of the bar beneath the head of a nail and pry.

As the gravedigger pushed down on the lever the nail grew from the wood with an almost human groan, and Nick saw Malena's shoulders move at the sound. Now another nail cried and Nick looked away. His eyes fell on the wooden cross on the ground next to the grave as another nail screamed, and he wondered whether his father had died quietly.

The old gravedigger paused in his work, removed his cracked straw hat, and pulled his sleeve across his dry forehead in an exaggerated, theatrical way, which made Nick think of the glint of pride in his eye as he smoothed the mortar to seal away Barbarita's body.

Once again the gravedigger hooked the crowbar under the lid and pulled. The lid moved an inch and the old man worked the tool around the edge of the coffin clockwise, turning in a complete circle until all the nails were pulled free. Then he slid the curved end of the tool under one side of the lid and, as Nick held his breath, raised it as though opening a door to meet the man residing inside.

As light fell on the dead man within, Malena put her hand to her mouth and gasped, the old gravedigger looked up to Hernandez with a confused gaze, and Nick took in a deep, quick breath and turned away, feeling suddenly dizzy and sitting abruptly on the mound of earth that had been lifted from the grave.

Hernandez stood with hands on hips, moving his head from side to side as he stared at the corpse of a thin, dark-skinned campesino half Professor Petrov's age. A sparrow trilled from the cottonwood tree. The police chief tugged at his belt and spoke.

"Señora Gonzalez will be pleased to learn that I have finally located her missing husband."

Malena looked to Nick, who sat with his back to the grave, elbows resting on his knees, hands hanging free between his legs. Hernandez also looked at him with pursed lips then turned back to the grave-digger.

"You put the gringo in this grave?"

"Sí, Jefe. Sí."

"Seguro?"

"I am sure."

"Then dig deeper," Hernandez ordered.

"Mande?"

"More deep."

The old man stared at Hernandez, who nodded to reassure him he had not misunderstood. Then the gravedigger climbed from the grave and went to fetch the others to help him lift Gonzalez out of the way so he could get to the corpse of the gringo.

Despite the heat of the day, the night air hung cold. Malena had built a fire of mesquite in her chimenea and they sat before it, Nick leaning back on the cushions placed on the petate de palma, Malena sitting upright on the mat, legs folded to the side, gazing into the fire. He studied her, sipping at his brandy. Finally she spoke:

"Tell me, Nicholas, what is fire. What is it made of?"

As he shifted his gaze to the flames she went on:

"We can see its shape and feel its heat. But when we try to hold it, it is not there."

"Perhaps it's only an illusion, Malena. What we see may exist only in our minds."

"Still. . ."

She raised the thick glass to her lips and swallowed down some brandy, closing her eyes as she did so. Then without turning away from the fire she said, "No váyate. Don't go."

He looked her up and down then stared at his drink.

"I have to go. You know why I came. Now that I have my father's body I have to see him buried with my mother. That is what he wanted."

"When will you leave?"

"Mañana."

There was a pause, as though time had stopped for an instant. Then he saw her breathe out.

"When will you return?"

A question he had heard before. He had had no good answer for it when his wife had asked it and none now. He kept staring into his brandy, feeling Malena's eyes on him.

"Vamos a ver," he said. That was the best he could do: We will see.

Her eyes flashed and she opened her mouth to speak but did not. She turned back to the fire.

"I am going to have your baby."

Nick took a deep, painful breath.

"Perhaps this is true, Malena, but I do not think so. It's too soon to tell."

She looked at him. "But perhaps it is so. Then you must return to be the father of your child."

"Mira. I haven't thought on any of this. I didn't think about it when I first took you to my room. Maybe that was wrong, but a man is not made to think at such times. I came here for my father and now I'll return home with him. When that's finished then I can think more on this thing between us. But not now. Now I can promise nothing."

She shook her head slowly. "Nicholas, you never should have come."

"I had no choice, Malena. I was brought here." The fire cracked and he took a long drink of this brandy.

"Truly," said Malena. "In such things we do not choose. That is for the gods. We must follow the path they make for us without knowing our destination. But now your path and mine have met. We have a life to live together."

Vamos a ver, he thought, but could think of nothing to say that would help.

Malena set the brandy glass on the mat beside her then reached down to the front of her black dress where, one by one, she unfastened the buttons that ran its length. As she moved to him he felt the warmth of her against his chest and her breasts pressing against him and heard her breathe into his ear:

"Make love to me, Nicholas, as though it was the last time."

■

It came to him in a dream that seemed more a remembrance, rare and priceless time-traveling to an Eden lost. They were journeying together, the three of them. His father drove as verdant hills and trees, multi-colored flowers, and radiant waters streamed by outside the car's windows like a gaudy diorama. The aromatic smoke of his father's pipe hovered spirit-like over his mother. She held Nicholas in her lap, his ear against her breast listening to her heart, a fragrance of roses and sharp musk all about him, she looming over him with a palpable power, washing over his dream-mind and producing an agonizing longing. A myth woman who carried with her a sense of home and goodness long beyond his reach, an essence once in his own heart but that he had soiled with his own hands. . .Now he traveled alone through a barren, windblown landscape, dust and debris swirling, the rank smell of decaying flesh in his nostrils. His dream-mind now analytical: Life is but corruption, which few leave with clean hands—he looked down to blood-stained fingers—and which moves inexorably toward death. A specter of Death now came to him, black, invisible, a dark cloud of nothingness. Nick tried to turn away. "Not yet," he called, and fled across the desert in search of the dream family, of the journey through a sunny savanna, of the moment of joy.

Eighteen

Malena and he walked side by side up the hill from her casita, Nick carrying the worn leather suitcase he had arrived with. They turned onto the street that ran beside the market, where vendors sat idly beneath the canvas covers of their stalls waiting for someone who needed a bicycle pedal, cooking pot, or crucifix. An old campesino driving three burros up the street stopped and turned toward the couple as they passed, raising his straw hat.

At the corner they side-stepped another peasant who had apparently come in from the countryside to market whatever he had managed to pull from the earth and who now lay motionless face-down on the stone banqueta. From one back pocket of his dusty trousers protruded an empty Coke bottle, from the other a red-capped plastic container of pure alcohol. Nick saw Malena move around the man without so much as a glance, as if for her he did not exist.

As they turned the corner at the church a hand clamped onto Nick's arm. He stopped and whirled and saw a dark green sleeve. His eyes followed the sleeve up to the face of Raúl. Jaime stood just behind him and to his left. Raúl's reddened eyes smiled.

"Nicholas! Come have a drink. We worked all night and have finally succeeded. Now we are celebrating. I wish to invite you."

Nick managed a smile and looked to Jaime and back to Raúl. "Muchas gracias, pero. . ." He lifted his chin toward Malena standing beside him. The two soldiers touched their caps and bowed almost imperceptibly toward her.

"Then another time," said Raúl. "Whenever you wish, you will be our guest."

"Very kind. Gracias."

To be tendering such a gracious invitation, Nick mused, the two soldiers must have added something, somewhere, to their fifty cents a day. Perhaps that's what Raúl meant by their having finally succeeded. Perhaps they had finally succeeded with Luis and Miguel.

Raúl's eyes dropped to the suitcase in Nick's hand then looked up with an expression of seemingly genuine disappointment.

"You are leaving? Why? Where are you going?"

"I must travel for business. When I return we will drink a beer together."

"When?"

Nick felt Malena's eyes on him.

"Pronto. We will see each other."

"Sí. Nos vemos."

Nick and Malena moved on. When they were halfway down the block she said, "Those two are not gentlemen."

At the zócalo Nick set his suitcase on the stones beside one of the metal benches.

"Wait for me a moment."

He crossed the street to the police station and disappeared inside. When he returned ten minutes later Malena still stood beside the bench with arms folded.

They crossed together to the other side of the square and stood waiting by the taxi stand in the shade of an elm. Another ten, silent minutes passed as nearby a man polished shoes and sold lottery tickets to passersby. Finally Francisco drove up in his taxi and leaned out the window.

Nick and Malena climbed into the back seat of the cab, which moved out beyond the edge of town. They passed the fruit stand beneath the palms where the woman with the fly swatter still stood guard while across the road flies swarmed over a dead burro stiffening in the ditch.

When they got to the train station the hearse that had carried Barbarita's body to the panteón was backed up to the tracks, a fresh pine coffin visible through the side windows. Nick, Malena, and Francisco got out of the cab, the two men nodding to the driver leaning against the hearse.

Francisco waited by the taxi as Malena and Nick climbed the stairs to the station platform, where Malena stood in the shade under the eaves. Nick paced back and forth muttering to himself between steps. Be on time. Let's get this over with.

After a minute, as though reading his thoughts, Malena said, "Yo me voy. I am going."

As she moved toward the wooden steps leading from the platform Nick stepped in her path. She stopped and raised her eyes, looking at him as though she did not know him. But then she seemed to soften and reached up to touch his face.

"You are two people, Nicholas. The child you were born and the man you have become. But the child is your strength, for he is the sorcerer."

She turned away and moved rapidly down the steps. Francisco went to the back door of the taxi and grabbed the handle, but she walked past without looking at him, moving up the road away from the station with long strides.

Nick moved to the edge of the platform lifting his hand to his brow to shield the sun, watching her silhouette climb the hill. Halfway up, a dirty gray pariah that had been sleeping beneath a madroño tree rushed at her, barking and snapping. She kicked at the dog, which caused it to slink away. Malena disappeared over the hill.

Nick thought he felt the train approaching and turned away.

Epilogue

A green canvas roof had been erected over the grave but the morning rain had ceased. Now only a low, gray autumn sky hung overhead, as if pressing all into the ground.

On the other side of the grave stood the priest, white clerical collar visible beneath his overcoat and scarf, reading from the worn Bible in his hand. But the words came to Nick vaguely, as though from a great distance, his eyes darting unfocused about the tent, and he would not have been able to paraphrase one thing the man had said.

Nick stood with gloved hands folded in front of him, his wife beside him, her hand on the arm of his wool topcoat. Then he felt her squeeze his arm gently and looked up, realizing the priest had stopped speaking. Nick turned to the small group of people—his father's colleagues, largely—standing behind him.

"Thank you all very much for coming. . ."

He could think of nothing else to say.

Nick pulled off his right glove and shook hands with the mourners, remembering some of the faces dimly, seeing others for the first time, realizing that the man in the ground behind him had had another life about which he, the son, knew next to nothing. It was as though he were the outsider here. He grasped the hand of the final straggler.

"I'm Dr. Aaron Bergman. . ."

A man not even his own age. The new generation of archaeologists. Nick studied his face trying to recall it.

"I'm sorry, have we met?"

"No, I'm not one of your father's colleagues. I was treating him—I'm a cardiologist. When I saw the notice in the paper. . ."

At the word "cardiologist" Nick felt a rush of blood to his head. As long as he could remember, his father had gone only to Dr. Kaminski, his chess partner, and then only when Kaminski finally cajoled him into a check-up.

"Treating him?"

"Perhaps 'treating' isn't the exact word. I saw him only twice. But I did warn him about altitudes—that's high country there, isn't it, where he had his heart attack?"

Nick nodded. The second autopsy, performed once his father's body had been returned to the States, reconfirmed the phantom first: cardiac arrest. But it couldn't have told him this—the likely proximate cause of the attack. Nick now shook his head.

"Then he knew."

Bergman frowned. He was Nick's height and wore a black fedora that added a few years—the doctor was barely thirty. He now seemed uncertain, perhaps chastising himself for saying too much or anything at all.

"I specifically advised him about avoiding high altitudes, alcohol, overdoing it. But people don't always listen. You see it all the time, even with educated men like your father. They deny the scientific facts or refuse to follow orders for whatever reason. And it makes you feel bad, like you should have done more."

Nick shook his head. "No. Not your fault. You really couldn't tell him anything."

When Bergman had gone only Nick and his wife remained. He stood with hands clasped behind him, studying her as she stood shivering under the tent examining the headstone. He got her attention and lifted his chin toward the trees and dark grass in front of him. She nodded and took his arm and together they strolled over the damp earth.

He walked on his heels, looking at the ground, glancing at the names and dates on the stones; she tiptoed, careful not to catch the sharp heels of her black shoes in the thick grass. Nick raised his gaze to the low gray sky as he walked.

"Winter soon."

She nodded and said, "You did the right thing, Nick."

Still walking he turned to his wife, her off-blonde hair tucked beneath a black beret, downy wisps lying on the back of her long neck. Regan wore a black wool coat belted at the waist, and he thought how good she looked whatever the occasion. She always looked fine. But he wasn't sure what she had referred to, what right thing he had done. When he didn't respond she reiterated:

"It was the right thing to do, bringing him back. Otherwise you would have always felt you let him down. Now at least you know that everything was the way he wanted it."

Nick shook his head thinking that little between his father and him had ever gone the way his father wanted it. He reached inside his overcoat to pull out a pack of cigarettes. His father had known about his vulnerable heart and had chosen to ignore his doctor's warnings. Chose instead to go where he was likely to die—and where his son might follow. Where they had gone before, together, when Nicholas was a boy, before whatever they had had between them became lost or misplaced. Now Nick realized how important those trips together must have been to the old man.

He stopped and struck a match, cupping his hands against the wind. Soon a good tobacco smell swirled up to him. He inhaled and looked up into the tall pines that seemed almost to touch the hovering gray clouds.

"He knew about his heart. He went to the mountains where the air was thin, not to his dig in the Yucatan. He chose to die in Mexico knowing I would come."

Regan frowned and shook her head at her husband.

"You started smoking again? And after what happened to him? You know your mother died young, too."

He looked at her as though she were a stranger who spoke a different tongue. But he should have grown accustomed to it by now. She heard only what she wanted to hear. And Nick wondered if that wasn't what had warned his methodical father against her. He glanced down at the cigarette in his hand as if pondering how it got there. "Yeah, I guess I started again."

"You better take care of yourself, Nick."

"I will."

Again he took off the glove. They grasped hands and she pressed a cold cheek against his.

Nick stood smoking his cigarette under the pines, watching her tiptoe away to the black limousine waiting near the green tent.

Nick sat on the white wall-to-wall carpet, leaning against the bare wall, staring out the tall window of the empty apartment. Snow had begun to fall and he was thankful for it covering the gray city below. He sipped from a glass of vodka, took a pull on his cigarette, and crushed it out in an upturned mayonnaise lid on the floor next to him.

After a minute he reached for his pack of Faros on the floor beside the mayonnaise lid and found he had smoked the last one. He stood and moved to the suitcase lying open on the floor where the sofa had been, the black overcoat he had worn to the cemetery beside it on the white carpet.

Nick searched the suitcase, pushing aside rumpled shirts and jeans and his father's Bible. When his fingers grasped something hard he frowned, withdrew his hand, and gazed into the black, obsidian eyes of Miquitzli. He had forgotten about it but now remembered the night he woke from his dream of being buried alive in the desert, saw the death's head Vicente had given him sitting on the desk, and hid it away in the suitcase.

He turned the carving in his hand thinking of Vicente and of what he, Nick, had done. But instead of returning the death's head to its hiding place, he set Miquitzli on the carpet next to the ashtray as though to keep him company. He found another pack of Faros in the bottom of the suitcase and went back to sitting on the floor looking out the window.

He tapped the pack on the back of his hand, took a cigarette from it, and tossed the pack to the floor. After he lit up he poured more vodka into his glass and sipped. All gray, white, black. Now it seemed so odd to him. He recalled the colors—the gaudy flowers and pale green palms, the vermilion flycatcher, the blood.

As Nick reached up and pulled loose the black tie, unbuttoned the white shirt collar, and spread it open, his fingertips brushed the leather thong around his neck. He pulled on it and laid the amulet in the palm of his hand. He took another drink of vodka, studying the carved jade.

Kukulcan. Quetzalcoatl. The plumed serpent. The snake that can fly and leave its earthly existence. And he saw now in his mind the moment he had seen it first—when he pulled the red dress off over her head and the green amulet lay between her dark breasts like a charm to ward off evil, or as an invitation to something unknown or long forgotten—and his breath seemed to catch in his chest.

Nick rubbed the jade with his thumb—back and forth, back and forth—as though to release the magic to which his father had summoned him and that, in turn, now called him.